Swimming Between Two Waters

Swimming Between Two Waters

THE MORNING OF THE MOGUL: PART III. BOOK 10.

Hichem Karoui

Global East-West (London)

Contents

Dedication

To the memory of Nana …
Beloved mother...
You are always in my heart.
May you rest in eternal peace.

Notes

Note of the Publisher

This is Mister Bassam Bourasin's admitted report as a citizen of His republic. He didn't give it a name. He initially addressed it to the Interior Ministry. Instead, it landed on my desk. I publish it as is, with no major changes to its form or content. However, because the report is around 800 pages long, it was serialised and divided into three parts. The two previous parts have already been published.

Here comes book Ten, ending Part III (*Dolce Vita*) and the novel.

I also noticed that this is a translation. The first draft was written in Arabic. The author had no intention of publishing it. In any case, it is understandably unpublishable in the country... for the same reasons that silence any samizdat in the Arab world today, like yesterday!

Hichem Karoui

Note of the Author

All of the individuals in my story, as well as the country, are not made up. However, even if some characters claim to be more fictive or strange, crazier or more foolish than others, they are not required to justify their location. My country can be found throughout the Arab world. Whatever name people give it, you won't notice a difference if you pay attention.

Bassam Bourasin

The Morning of the Mogul: Part III

DOLCE VITA

Book 10:
Swimming Between Two Waters

One

I returned to my hotel enraged, confused, and almost frustrated since I couldn't get my hands on them despite having two hundred thousand dollars. Hassan gave me the number for my new bank account but cautioned me that I could not withdraw the entire amount immediately; he kept the cheque with him, assuming that I might lose it.

"What, after all, are you going to do with all that money?" He said. "You don't need it right now because we pay the hotel's bill."

"But I signed the contract," I objected.

"You signed it, and I'm not denying your rights." Your money is secure, but you must wait for the government to pay. These are not a trifling modicum, but two hundred million dollars. We must obtain the approval of the Minister of Finance, as well as the Central Bank and the President. So please wait."

"I am not claiming $200 million."

"Not you, lad, but the firm with which you're working. You'll cash your cheque once everyone else has been paid. Don't be concerned; you saw the contract, didn't you? The British company is real, the helicopters are in the Ministry's yard, and the money is somewhere between our Central Bank, Switzerland, and London."

"I know the helicopters are here since I saw one on my way to the Ministry. I am, however, a little hazy. Why do we need three banks to close the deal?"

"You're always asking questions you shouldn't be asking. Do you really need to know everything? Assume that a portion of the payment was made through a Londoner bank and that we now require the services of a Swiss banker to move our funds to London. How did you get it?"

"Sir, that was not in the contract I signed."

"What exactly do you mean?"

"I'm referring to the first instalment of payment. In fact, the contract is explicit: the entire payment will be made after we receive the helicopters."

That enraged him. He didn't want me to know anything else about that bid.

"Take a look here, little chap. I'm not going to allow you to investigate my business. You signed your page and got your cheque; the rest is no longer your responsibility. Whether we pay the firm in two, three, or five instalments is none of your business. Your role in the game is to sign anything I give you, keep your mouth sealed, and wait for more instructions. Is that clear?"

"Sir, yes."

He calmed down. After a time, he inquired if I needed anything. I hesitated for a second, then admitted that I needed some cash for my expenses and was afraid of the return of a blank cheque.

"A blank cheque? Do you yearn for the menagerie? How much is it?"

"Oh! It was for a good cause, sir, the Medina Association of Safeguard. 4000..."

" 4,000 what?"

"Four thousand dollars, Sir."

"We'll call you double-headed saint!"

"Too much kind of you, Sir."

"Come on, be serious. Those guys are wealthier than you, me and the Minister together. How do you believe they have reached the top in a few years? Just asking for donations from saints like you and telling them the story of making the poor and the homeless happy. As it happens, there are more poor and homeless people every day, and they are not happy, I can tell you. Look, my friend, God, not you and me, is responsible for those unhappy. He created them, threw them in this country, and then decided to give all the wealth to other people who do not necessarily deserve it. It's just the lottery! What can we do?"

Such a comment coming from an official in the Islamist government astounded me. If it turned out to be accurate, it wasn't good. I wasn't sure whether I should believe him or not. But I cannot believe that God could be evil. As I did not answer, he went on:

"I'm unsure if you're too honest or blind!" He exclaimed. "Really! Should I keep you under constant monitoring 24 hours a day so you can learn to distinguish who is your friend and who is deceiving you? Here is the bank account number. Accept it. I deposited $10,000 into your account, which you can use as you see fit. Nonetheless, I recommend that you exercise caution rather than throwing your money out the window. What the hell! Try to be a wise man! You are lucky since you have two heads in one. Use one of them at least!"

Saying this, he burst into laughter, happy with his silly joke.

This conversation occurred just after the brief interview with the Minister. The latter had been pleasant and courteous, and I immediately realised that his face was not unfamiliar to me. He was short, obese, and bald; his tiny eyes sparkled, and his mouth was ringed by a trim beard covering only his chin. He was dressed stylishly and spoke quickly with a harsh voice and in hushed tones, emphasising some words clearly and audibly, such as state, government, Islamic Revolution, and half-swallowing his statements as though the other words were useless to him.

"Wecom'ster'ssam," he began as we shook hands, which I translated as "Welcome Mister Bassam," and he went on to say, "I no a ged del bout yeh, thaks to ster'ssan who tak of yeh s' his man'f confidence."

I thanked him profusely, emphasising how honoured I was to meet a historical figure of the Islamic State, and he didn't waste time: "Think you keepin up well with Government the Islamic Revolution; vrythin owever's based on trust a confidence a secrecy; a you no of coss the cost of the bellion in guns, men, moey. We nee a let of money an guns and of coss aliable men, an discreet, an..."

I intercepted the last sentence and decoded it: "We need money, weaponry, and trustworthy men who are also discreet."

There was a lot of whistling and hissing, but he continued his voluble stammering, and I could hardly extricate anything intelligible. I just wondered how his subordinates or even his colleagues understood what he was hopelessly trying to say in his burbling language, but they're probably used to it. Then it hit me. This was the silent man I had seen in the restaurant, dining with that rowdy group of officers. He certainly didn't notice me, even though I had been pretty conspicuous, lighting Mrs Waterbird's cigarette and engaging in jittery, airy talk with her. Anyway, I held off on bringing up the matter because he said nothing.

Finally, he stood up, signalling the audience's time had ended. It had lasted perhaps ten or fifteen minutes, during which he was the principal soloist in a completely hazy symphony written by a mad brain, prey to the greatest disorientation.

I had told the chauffeur that I would return to the hotel after a short walk through the streets. My meeting with the Minister and his Director of Security did not improve my mood. I was being pushed to the limit, yet I was conscious that if something went wrong, I could be blamed. Neither Hassan nor his Minister would admit to planning every element of that phoney agreement, leaving me to bear the penalties and face prosecution alone. I was their stooge and was starting to realise that the game was outwitting me. I walked aimlessly in the crowded streets, battered by the blazing sun, impotent and resigned.

I walked into a coffee shop, tripped over a chair, and ordered a black coffee. I lit a cigarette and stared aimlessly down the street. I felt the despair of the crowd penetrating me more than ever before. It was like a poison leaking into the city's atmosphere, pouring from every face, invading every corner, sticking like a rigid glue even to the seats, tables, and walls, engulfing everyone around me and infecting my thinking. I was burdened by a discouraging commitment that made me feel helpless, as if I were sinking in a vast sea of horrible malevolence. The dismal discontent of those anonymous faces penetrated my psyche and made me feel bitter and entirely shattered by grudging dismay. I was depressed. All those eyes appeared to stab me accusingly as if they were all well aware of my guilt, and the mouths seemed to mutter and insinuate that I was a fool... a fool who accepted to engage in a game that would not only overtake him but would eventually destroy him. Where has your wisdom gone, man? Don't you see that Hassan and his Minister make you seem foolish? Do you feel guilty or embarrassed? Guilty or ashamed? Yes, maybe, but not for what I did at the Ministry. I was still thinking about when I was alone with the lovely Mrs Waterbird in the lift and... Oh my goodness! If I keep going in this direction, I'll end up in a mental institution!

I jumped to my feet and stormed towards the gate. I didn't turn my head or halt when I heard the waiter behind me say, "Your coffee, Sir..." I couldn't tolerate the stench of hatred, aggressiveness, looming violence, and similar unpleasant sensations. People appeared to be resentful of their government. I didn't see a smiling face in the entire bloody city, and I overheard some of them insulting and ridiculing officials without naming them. I've never liked the capital, but since I have to live there, I should strive to avoid such pointless and dangerous situations. It is extremely risky to be seen sitting next to a group of provocateurs vilifying the administration, which will happen again if I do not exercise caution. Indeed, I do not share these extremist beliefs since, by habit, I am always loyal to the government. Nonetheless, I don't need to give anyone a reason to suspect me. I know from personal experience that our police ears are pretty sensitive. In addition, I am now almost a public figure; I hobnob with government members. I have the finest intentions for the little people of this city, with whom I sympathise entirely and unreservedly. I know they are for nothing in the confluence of tragic incidents that brought the country from disaster to devastation. Alas! I am as powerless as they are. Furthermore, I am attempting to assist them. I gave a $4,000 cheque to a charity that helps the homeless. True, the cheque was a fake, but my intentions remain the best in the world.

***

After a short nap, I visited Mr Waterbird's artistic exhibition in the afternoon. The gallery was almost empty. A few kids, maybe three or four, spread about the large space, and they didn't appear particularly enthralled by that type of painting. Mr Waterbird appeared to be napping in an armchair, an open book on his thighs, and his belly undulating softly with his breathing. I approached him cautiously and saw he was snoring. Happy man!

I took a space tour, paying close attention to the paintings. I didn't grasp much of what was represented in that joyful splattering and splashing of colours, shades, and lights. But I overheard one of the kids say to his friend, "Did you see the title of this canvas?" "Donkey's tail!"

"Funny!"

"It means he bathed his donkey's tail in colour and stuck it over the canvas."

"Ingenious!"

"Yeah, but if a donkey can do it with its tail, the donkey is the painter, not the man."

"Perhaps it wasn't the donkey that did it, the second young man speculated.

" So, who did?"

" The painter is most likely the guy you see there. But you wouldn't detect a difference between his work and the animal's. So, they are partners."

The two laughed heartily. I turned to watch Mr Waterbird, but he was still snoozing, indifferent to his triumph.

At that time, his lovely wife walked in, spotted me, smiled, and rushed to greet me warmly: "Oh! "Thank you for coming, Mister Bassam." She turned around, surprised, and shouted, "Oh! What happened? How long have you been here?"

I informed her that I just arrived.

" It's odd! The gallery seems so sad, she continued. It was so crowded in the morning that you couldn't even walk. People crowded around the pictures, some queuing in the corridor, and Robert felt compelled to speak to everyone."

"That seemed to have exhausted him, I said, pointing to the snoring man, and now he's having a short nap."

I didn't believe anything she said. Even in peacetime, before the last insurgency, the country was not much concerned about painting exhibitions and culture. We have crowded mosques but hardly crowded art exhibitions. There are local painters, but they live on the state's charity. How about now, after the Islamist regime has settled down? What puzzles me is not that the gallery was almost empty but that it was still open for exhibitions. The only reason I can think of is that nobody knows about it among the new officials, who should be more preoccupied with the civil war than with artists and exhibitions.

" He's pretty solicited right now. We're going on a European tour soon. We received invitations from folks in Paris, Rome, Berlin, and even Moscow. You won't believe it, Mr Bassam, but we are literally overwhelmed."

"I can imagine, Madam."

She was wearing a short-sleeved white silky shirt over a black skirt, and I immediately noticed the several bracelets encircling her wrist because she was speaking with her hands - and it seemed to me with her entire body - gesticulating and somewhat bestowing her proponent and firm breasts as to emphasise her words. Obviously, she disliked seeing her husband sprawled and comfortably snoozing in his armchair, oblivious to the rest of the world. She raised her eyebrows at him briefly, then crossed the distance separating us from the sleeping man and pinched his arm.

"Robert! She exclaimed."

He opened his eyes wide and mumbled, "Who? What?"

"Look who's here, dear, she said, all honey. This is Mister Bourasin; isn't it gracious of him to come?"

I took a step forward and then stood beside her. The painter gave me a cool gaze:

"Ah! Welcome!"

I smiled, hoping to persuade him to speak more... in vain! 'Ah, welcome,' it appears, was his best effort in conversation. Mrs Waterbird asked me:

"Did you see the pictures? We'll show you around. Robert would love to guide you. Are you coming, Robert?"

I doubted he could string two phrases together, but he trailed us meekly, breathing heavily and almost wobbling. We stopped in front of a large canvas striped laterally by a progression of colours representing all possible variants of green and blue.

"This is the achromatic scale, she explained. I particularly enjoy it because of the admirable proportion of light and shadow. He worked on it for several months while also painting other pictures."

The explanation she provided me untangled the conundrum without revealing all of its hidden knots. I murmured to myself that it is never too late to further one's education, but I inquired about the price because I was probably expected to say something.

"It's not expensive, she said. Unfortunately, this one is already sold. I'm sorry! However, you might come across something different and no less interesting. I'm not only Robert's wife but also his agent. If you're ready to invest, I can advise you... For example, a painting of 'dead nature' or a 'flower pot' would look great in an office, unless you prefer something for your home. In this case, I recommend the 'donkey's tail'... "

I glanced at the last painting, wondering why it had been so strangely titled; to me, it represented nothing more than a splatter of unspecifiable colours. I am not a connoisseur; there is no reason to act like one. I looked at the artist, following us hesitantly and pondered if he was absent or with us. He didn't say anything. Honestly, I wasn't expecting him to. I already knew he couldn't say much more than 'Ah, welcome,' even if we were together all afternoon and into the evening.

" Well, it's... uh... quite... ahem... colourful", I said.

" You're not going to believe it, Mr Bassam. A banker in Geneva spotted this canvas and wanted to buy it. He is an amazing collector who used to visit European galleries in search of rare gems of modern painting. He said, "I recognised Robert's talent at first sight, and this painting is truly a gem." She added emphatically that he would have bought it even if I had asked for £20,000 or more...

"So, didn't you sell it?" I inquired.

"Robert declined." She chuckled.

I couldn't believe a donkey's tail was worth £20,000 or more, although I wasn't sure if she was talking seriously or to make a point. In any case, it was clear that Robert wanted his tail to stay with him.

"Who would think twice about making a deal at that price?" I said.

"This is because you're a businessman, Mr Bassam. You realise that a good opportunity should be seized."

"Right, I'm always looking for good opportunities."

"Well, here's an opportunity for you, Mr Bassam. Don't let it go. I'll sell you this canvas for only £ 2 thousand. Robert has finally decided to sell it, and trust me, it was difficult to persuade him."

She smiled softly and pushed her fascinating bosom proudly forward.

'If she keeps doing this,' I told myself, 'she'll make me broke as quickly as she made me nuts! I possess $200,000. Is it reasonable to spend them even before cashing my cheque?'

I don't deny that I was mesmerised by Mrs Waterbird's charm, but her chiaroscuro confounded me, and I struggled to keep my head clear and cool. I didn't want to appear stingy, which I am not, and I didn't want to buy such an expensive donkey's tail. In any case, where would I place it? I have neither an office nor a house away from my dear 'Ouja.

"I think you should sell it to the Geneva banker. Twenty thousand is genuinely a deal. I cannot offer you a more significant price, and I would feel tremendously bad and ashamed if I accepted this authentic work for much less than its actual value. Please, trust me. I enjoy this piece of art but can't afford it right now. Accepting your generous offer would make me feel like a thief. Besides, I understand that Mr Waterbird is extremely attached to this canvas, and I don't want to steal it from him at such a low price."

I heard a short laugh and turned to find Mr Waterbird making every attempt to cut off what appeared to be an unexpected burst of hilarity. He huffed, gasped, coughed, panted, attempting to hide his face with that incredible mirth; but finally, incapable of more restraint, he came out in a piercing diluvial laughing.

I was perplexed and stared at him, as his wife glared and said loudly, "Robert! Robert!" "What the hell is going on?"

She then turned to me, ashamed, and apologised, "Sorry Mr Bassam; he is having his crisis. Because of all this exhausting activities, it had been expected for days."

I tried to smile, but she seemed glum, and my smile likely turned into a scowl.

"What's your point, Robert? Is it necessary to whoop and

whack right now? Ok, since you're so delighted, do it yourself. I'm not interested anymore."

She then turned to face me, apologised, and took leave.

"Janet, where are you going?" Yelled Mr Waterbird, who had gathered himself again, as she hurried towards the door.

She didn't seem to care and continued strolling down the corridor.

" Sorry, Mr. Robert, she seems angry, I said and prepared to go.

His hand waved in a sign of indifference.

"Yeah! Never mind, she can go. She lost her sense of humour. She's bloody incapable of laughing at nothing."

Finally, I was relieved to notice that he spoke like everyone else. However, I must admit I didn't understand the joke either. I couldn't determine whether to be happy for his speech recovery or sorry for the irritated wife's quick departure.

"Please accompany me, Mr Bassam. Let's have a drink together. I'm incredibly thirsty, and drinking only fruit juice and cold water is a nightmare. Such infantile behaviour does not sit well with me. Come on, sir, I have plan B for such occasions."

I wanted to apologise and escape, but I couldn't refuse such a kind request. Since I was waiting for him to speak, I was curious to hear what the silent man had to say. So, I followed him into a little room adjacent to the gallery, which I had not noticed.

The area appeared to be an anteroom for the artist's private usage. He turned on the lights because the curtains were covering the window. At the far end of the room was a couch, a desk, and two chairs in the centre. To my surprise, Mr Waterbird unlocked a cupboard and pulled out a bottle of Whisky and two glasses. Amid prohibition, threats, and witch-hunting, the sight of that bottle filled me with horror and misery. Bewildered, I was about to flee. But his soft voice calmed my terror and captivated me. The devil's temptation was too strong to resist.

"Of course, it's prohibited, Mr Bassam. But not drinking in this climate is a greater sin. Please accept my apologies for the lack of ice cubes, but I do have some mineral water."

I wasn't sure. Would I risk being lashed and jailed by the militia if I touched the forbidden thing again, although it had been long since I hobnobbed with Bacchus? Everything has changed. Gangs of men armed with sticks and cudgels patrol the streets of the capital and other cities and villages, bringing anybody who breaks their law on his knee.

"No, thank you, Mr. Waterbird," I was about to say when my hand flew out of control and gripped the glass half-full of the bright, yellow liquid. In no time, as if afraid of being caught with the evidence of my crime, I hastened to gulp it down, somewhat to get rid of it like a bitter but necessary medicine, while telling myself, 'Allah will forgive me no doubt, even if the men are merciless'! Mr Waterbird slapped my back and murmured, "Slowly, slowly." Nobody will ever know."

He filled my glass when I asked for water. My neck and entire bosom were on fire. I drank whisky with Hamda La'war and Haj Mukhtar several times, and still, I can't resist it. I sipped the water.

"Either this isn't regular whisky, or I've never truly drunk it, Mr Waterbird."

He burst out laughing.

"I recommended softening it with water, but you refused.

I'm sorry; I understand that with their heinous prohibition, all you want is a drop of booze. But don't worry, Mr Bourasin; the source will not dry; there are two more bottles... If I may say so, ha ha ha... well hidden from the devil's view."

"If you don't want to get into trouble, you should hide them away. They'll lash you for a beer."

He served me another whisky, which I mixed with water.

"To your health!"

We drank.

I proposed a toast to the British Prime Minister, but he declined.

"What's the harm?"

"I did not vote for him," he said.

"Aha! Then let us drink for the health of the Shadow Prime," I replied.

"Not sure I'll vote for him either."

We laughed and sipped. The booze was good, and we cheered up.

We raised our glasses in tribute to British painters, the Archbishop of Canterbury, the Islamic Republic's Mufti, and even President Abdelghani Abdelghaffar.

"Had we... hick... fuck... hick hick... forgotten anyone? "

"Perhaps the Islamic Militia," I figured.

"Whatever! The devil takes them to... hick... hell! Hick!"

***

We drank much more. After closing the room's door, we took a comfy seat on the canapé. I'd finally overcome my nerves and felt entirely at ease with Robert Waterbird, and the whisky had removed our inhibitions. Then he told me that he didn't like what was happening in my country, which he had visited several times.

"I don't like it, either, I said, but I'm about to be decked..."

"Really? He exclaimed, Interlocked! How? For what?"

"How? I suppose, by the President himself. I am a national hero."

"Oooh! You! Robert's pupils dilated. Are you kidding me?"

" I'm dead serious."

He couldn't stop giggling. It was another of his unexpected bursts of laughing, and I joined in. He then recommended toasting "the intoxicated hero of the Islamic Republic"!

"That will not do! I fired back."

"Why not?"

"I'm unsure whether such a man exists in our country."

" Ha Ha! That's you, lad! Said he, almost choked with laughter."

I laughed and said

– Sorry! I didn't recognise myself initially, but now I am sure it's me."

We lifted our glasses.

" Yet, you don't know everything," I added.

"Certainly... hick... I'm not that super-powerful... hick!"

" Do you realise? I'm now a new rich."

" Ha, ha, ha! Janet informed me. That's outdated... hick... news. She knows... hick hick... everyone here... They say you're the new butt full of shit..."

"Janet? She knows her stuff."

"There's nowhere to hide in this... hick... bloody hotel."

"Not even a new butt full of shit! Ha Ha!"

" He He! By definition... hick... a new butt full of shit ... hick... is the most indiscreet thing on the planet... Ha Ha... It can't be hidden."

" It isn't a bottle of booze..."

We laughed.

" I'll buy some of your paintings because you're a brother, even though you're a terrible painter."

" How much?"

" Do you want to know the price?"

"Nay, how much terrible?"

"Oh! Enough to make you unable to paint a donkey's tail... Ha Ha!"

"Hick... Ha Ha... That's because you're blind. "

"How much blind?"

"Enough to make you unable to recognise a donkey's tail from his head... Ha Ha Ha!"

He was laughing so hard that he collapsed on the ground.

"You bloody drunk, Bassam... Hick... You don't want me to paint a stupid animal's tail. Anyway, Hick! You won't recognise it! Hick Hick!"

"I will. Hick! But you can't sketch a pig or a cow, and Hick! Your canvasses are as expensive as gold and diamonds! Hick!"

"Gold and diamonds! Ha Ha! That's what they are! Hick!"

" I'll give you a $1,000 cheque right now if you draw a cow in front of me with four legs, a tail, a head and everything else that makes it a cow. He He He!"

"Keep your dollars, tycoon. Hick! You'll lose them anyway, since Hick... they're useless to the ignorant... Hick! Butt full of shit!"

We laughed.

"I want a cow, Robert. Please, make me a cow..."

" Nay... Hick... There are enough cows and donkeys on the planet to... Hick!"

He took the bottle again. I said:

" Syphoned!"

We laughed.

"You're still thirsty!"

"Hick! We should ask the... Hick... fucking manager to open some bottles from the cellar."

"You're on the moon!"

"We can pay... Hick..."

"This is an Islamic country now. Ali Baba's cellar is illegal."

"Do you mean... Hick... Ali Baba's cellar was in Europe? The fucking caliphs... Hick... weren't drinking...Hick... in Bag... Hick Hick... Bagdad?"

"And Damascus..."

"And Hick... Mecca..."

We laughed.

"So, now that you'll be... Hick... decked... He He He... Inquire with... Hick.. His Excel... Hick... excellency. His cellar's indeed better equipped...Hoo Hoo Ha Ha He He!"

He was shaking and jerking again on the canapé.

"Don't be a fool, Robert. The President isn't a drunkard like you."

"What about you? Hick! Are you anything like me? Drunkard! Ha Ha Ha Ha... Hick!.... So... Hick Hick... Islamic hero! Hoo Hoo!"

"Bring another bottle. It's better."

" Yeah... How about Janet?"

"What have we got to do with her?"

"She's ... Hick... watching."

"What exactly is she watching? Do you mean she doesn't know about the booze?"

" She's... Hick... aligned with the fucking... Islamists! Hick! He exclaimed, shaking his head."

We laughed again.

"Does that mean she won't let us drink?"

"The bitch! Hick! Ha Ha! Doesn't even suspect..."

"Well, well, well! You cheated, didn't you?"

"Nope! She did... Hick! Aligned with the fucking... Hick... Islamists!"

We exchanged quiet glances before bursting out laughing.

"Let's have some coffee then," I suggested.

" Nay, go on your own... I'll stay here... Hick! I'm going to sleep."

He then spread out his legs, closed his eyes, and, in a few seconds, was already snoring on the couch. I opened the door and left.

***

Fortunately, the booze had not completely taken away my senses. I still could reason. So, I didn't go to the coffee shop because I was too inebriated to make the effort, and I was afraid of being seen staggering in the corridors. I'm not sure how long I was confined with Robert in that tiny room; probably the entire afternoon, because when I got back to my room, it was already dark and I had to switch on the light. Then I sprawled on the bed and promptly fell asleep.

The voice of the Muezzin summoning the faithful to the

prayer pulled me out of my dreams. I opened my eyes, believing it was the afternoon prayer because the room was brightly lit. But when I looked out the window, I realised it was daybreak. A murky blue surrounded the buildings, and the white stars in the sky were blinking. It was not the sun that illuminated my room. I have just neglected to turn off the electric bulb. As I tried to remember what happened, I felt my head engulfed by a thick fog. I stretched out my hand to the bedtable and switched off the light. The room returned to the darkness. I looked for my cigarettes but couldn't find them on the bedside table, so I touched myself and found that I was fully dressed: jacket, trousers, and shirt... I haven't even removed my shoes. The packet of cigarettes was completely torn up. Not surprising! However, two cigarettes were not entirely useless. I decided to smoke one of them and keep the other for emergency state.

Using a foot over the other, I pushed my shoes away, threw my jacket on the chair and started smoking. I was laying in bed, trying to recall the events of the previous day. I soon realised I would not return to sleep. So I smoked the second cigarette and got up. I stood up for a long time behind the window's glass, observing the dawn on the city's roofs.

The stillness had nearly come to an end. Apart from a few groups of soldiers or militiamen moving around, the streets were still deserted. I stood for another few moments behind the window glass before opening it. The early morning air entered the room and chilled me. I could hear an automobile engine receding away. I'm not sure why I immediately thought of Mr Waterbird's painting as the sky's extremes grew rosy and vivid. I was returning from a foggy and flustered world when it struck me that the entire city, as seen from this balcony at that early or late hour, that was neither morning nor night, was just as involved in a quiet struggle for life and light as some of Mr Waterbird's jumbled topics. Nothing but the static and enduring masses of the buildings, the fleecy and flexible shapes of the foliage and the trees, the fuzzy forms of the windows and bannisters half-sinking in semi-darkness could be discerned in that spilling and rigid stacking up of shades and lights. Then I understood what the artist was struggling to express.

The abstraction of the cities that Mr. Waterbird depicted is the secret I was unable to fathom, although his perspective was clearer and his understanding more compelling than what I could ever fully grasp. The ability to capture the essence of forms, lights, and colours in such a way was unfamiliar to me, given my accustomed interaction with a world that leans heavily toward materialism, leaving little room for an alternative perspective to filter through its confines. His vision remains unclouded by immediate needs and unaffected by the constraints of routine. Moreover, Mr. Waterbird's apparent lack of concern was, in truth, an undisturbed calm. This tranquillity of his soul allowed him to attain an understanding of the extraordinary world that had perpetually eluded me. This is why I perceived him to be content, quite possibly happier than myself—indeed, he was.

I settled myself into a contemplative state, poised to inscribe the chronicles of my days. I embarked upon formulating the embryonic framework of my most cherished endeavour. The tome I had acquired yielded a trove of captivating materials. It elucidated, among other tenets, that to be deemed 'Islamic,' financial institutions must earnestly enact the celestial doctrines proscribing usurious commerce and gains amassed through dormant capital. This necessitated the practical implementation of the tenet of exchange with a 'modest surplus,' elevated to the echelons of equitable value and weight, all within the purview of the cooperative doctrine governing the impartial apportionment of communal wealth. This, it asserted, was an indispensable prerequisite for the enduring opulence of the banks themselves and the amelioration of the quality of life for the 'Muslim Umma.' This community, poised to embrace transformative reforms grounded in moral and technical cooperative values, was to find a resolution to its economic, social, and financial quandaries solely through coalescent action. In my private journal, I assumed the mantle of authorship with gravitas, capturing the essence of this intricate discourse.

An auspicious beginning it presented, a prelude brimming with potential. Yet, the entire text demanded my undivided attention; its essence I sought to distill, the author's captivating turns of phrase poised to adorn my summation. As weariness set in, my notes found refuge within the recesses of a wardrobe concealed beneath layers of attire. With resolve, I embarked upon the grooming routine, the sound of cascading water mingling with the radio's broadcast. Through the airwaves, the announcement resonated—a triumphant Islamic Army, their might asserted, quashing insurrectionists as they attempted an assault on yet another hamlet. Thus, the spectre of a devastating massacre was averted; casualties and captives were the rebels' toll. Furthermore, a bounty of $200,000 was proffered, a reward for aiding the apprehension of the elusive Scoundrel.

Curious, the sum arrested my thoughts—why precisely $200,000? Mused I, was it but a mirror to the remuneration offered for my hand in facilitating the government's procurement of twice identical helicopters? Puzzlement clung to me, woven into an intricate tapestry of coincidence, as I hastened my ablutions, the radio silenced.

***

Two

At a later hour, while savouring my breakfast within the restaurant's ambience, a sight caught my attention: Mrs Waterbird, donned in a resplendent gown of pale yellow, gracefully approached. A wave of my hand signalled my presence, although she had already spotted me and made her way toward me, lips curving in a gentle dance and a smile gracing her visage.

"Good morning, Mr. Bassam."

"Good morning, Janet. Are you alone? Please, join me."

Seating herself adjacent to me, she chose a chair, not foremost, proximity that contented and gratified my being. My plate adorned with broiled eggs, I was already halfway with my breakfast. A waiter approached, and she placed an order for chilled chicken, eggs, milk, and a refreshing fruit elixir. With his departure, she asked:

"Why were you absent from the party yesterday? I presumed you had been invited, were you not?"

"The party? Ah, the gathering! Indeed... I, um, I must confess... it had escaped my mind. I apologise."

"Many intriguing individuals attended; the city's illustrious socialites, you know. It was a refined affair, replete with a lottery. I procured one of their tickets."

"May fortune favour you!"

"Robert, too, was a no-show. He was in quite a pitiable state; we quarreled again in the evening. He feigned illness, though I detected the scent of whiskey. Wherever did he unearth such spirits in this locale?"

I, a picture of feigned innocence, intoned with a sage-like air.

"Truly? A misunderstanding, perhaps. He might have consumed a tainted batch of lemonade that brought about his ailment..."

"Ah, ah, ah!" Her interjection interrupted my explanation. "I'm no fool; the distinction between whiskey and lemonade remains within my purview. He was indisputably inebriated, and I bristled at the prospect of his indiscretion being witnessed, thereby inviting potential censure."

"The Christians are afforded the liberty of imbibing," I ventured.

"Perhaps. Certainty eludes me. Given our countrymen's distressing alignment with the opposing president, I harbour reservations that the Capital's authorities would tolerate a tipsy drunkard parading unashamedly within their grandest establishment—even if the reveler in question were Picasso himself!"

"Are you referring to your compatriots stationed at the southern oil fields?"

"Exactly! Do you not peruse the news? The Islamists cast threats to assail those safeguarding the Scoundrel. And who fulfills this role, if not the Europeans and Americans?"

"No," I countered, "your interpretation is askew; the threats target the tribes providing him sanctuary, not the foreigners. In any case, the audacity to bomb your countrymen, even if complicit with the Scoundrel, shall not arise. They have no inclination to provoke Western reprisals, for all their zeal beckons them toward confrontation."

"Is that so? Indeed?"

"Yes."

She pondered a while, then voiced her thoughts.

"Perhaps, yet considering the grievous 'Ouja massacre...'"

"'Ouja,' you mean?"

"Indeed, 'Ouja!' A premonition of the direst outcome arises; the expulsion of all Westerners from the land would not astound me."

"Your outlook veers toward pessimism; it's worth noting I hail from 'Ouja, Janet."

Her gaze shifted as if seeing me anew or perhaps beholding a phantom.

"You? Good heavens! A survivor? My deepest condolences!"

"I've known the loss of both my mother and my betrothed in that tragedy."

I let this sentence trail off almost without thinking as if the words had lost their meaning in my head. Janet remained silent. Instead, she did something that was far more reassuring than any flippant sentence: she did something that I will never forget. She reached out and touched my shoulder as she looked at me with immense compassion. It was a spontaneous act, so human and friendly that it struck me deeply. Her white, warm hand rested gently on mine, and her fingers extended to me all the calming sympathy she could muster. Soon, I was overcome by conflicting emotions as I experienced heat waves and secretly hoped that her hand would never leave mine. However, the tender moment was over once the waiter returned with her breakfast, and she withdrew her warm hand. Then I cursed the waiter, and for the first time in my life, I wished that a man in good health would go down hit by a stroke!

After he left, I said, "Never mind!" Sometimes, you have to take a hit in life."

She retorted, "It's unfair."

"Nothing we do will make a difference."

I attempted to change the conversation as her mood deteriorated, asking, "Have you sold many pictures?"

She pondered as though this were the very last question anyone could ask.

"Yes, many pictures..." For a moment, she was silent. "I told you the exhibition is a success."

"Come now, Janet; I don't believe it."

She said nothing in response. I continued:

"I don't think you came over here at the correct time. The show is fine, but it feels out of place and time due to the war, the recession, and the devastation of so many people, not to mention the Islamists who have nothing to do with modern painting and don't even want to hear about it. Even though I am an art novice, I admire Robert and appreciate his efforts; he may be a talented painter, but this is not the ideal venue for his work.

There was an awkward pause in the conversation. The sun's rays were clustering and flooding into the ample space through the translucent glass that served as the wall separating the restaurant from the garden. Guests were seen strolling along the pool and lounging on the seats in the newly formed tree shade.

She dug around in her purse until she found her cigarettes, then she brought out a pack and stuck one between her full, pink lips. I lit it for her and then started one for myself. There weren't many people in the restaurant that early in the morning, and even though there were some Arab customers, they didn't pay any attention to us.

There was a plume of blue smoke as she declared, "Well, you won. Sorry, but I lied.

As I looked at her in silence, she added:

"I believed it was a blunder from the very beginning. I tried telling Robert the country was on fire, but he ignored me. He ignores whatever I say anyhow. When he sets up his mind about something, he is very unyielding. He was very familiar with the country and had always been welcomed. He didn't realise that the country he knew had changed so drastically that so many people were afraid for their safety and wouldn't even converse with us for fear of being labelled as British spies. He refused to concede that anything out of the ordinary had occurred; instead, he insisted on forming his own opinion based on what he saw with his own eyes. We hired the gallery for two weeks, but now we must cut it down to one week. That's terrible! We might as well have been in the desert, as is how sales are going. I thoroughly appreciate the hotel manager's anger at us for failing to inform him that our stay would be limited to one week. But we can't spend more money than we have, and if no one in this terrible country cares about modern art, that's not our problem. I'll admit that it wasn't always the case, but whatever good there was before has been lost in this awful war that saps resources and wears people out."

"Oh! You made no sales," I said.

She answered glumly, "Not a single picture."

I needed to soothe her now.

"Never mind, Janet," I said as I placed a hand on hers.

These were just some unfortunate circumstances that won't last forever.

She made a signature but didn't take it back afterwards, and her face showed no signs of emotion.

"Listen, Janet; whoever informed you that I am a millionaire is a liar. I'm not nearly as wealthy as most people think I am."

"But..."

I cut her off abruptly, saying:

"I knew this from Robert; you told him I am a tycoon, and he still thinks that. This is all a fabrication, Janet."

"Then you scammed every guest in this hotel, right? Are you perhaps a bit egotistical? What prompted all the rumours about your wealth?"

"It's the fact that those people are so thick-headed that they'll believe anything. Ultimately, I'll say it to myself, but it's nonsense. I don't deny that I'm working hard to make other people affluent or even more prosperous; if I can profit from that, it can't be all bad, right?"

"What are you doing, exactly?"

"Well, I am a kind of meddler between different people; I use their money to make them richer, I put them in contact with each other, and I take a commission."

"Is that person a business agent or stock broker?"

"Between the two extremes. For this reason, I propose we strike a deal."

I was being dishonest and truthful, but she still seemed intrigued.

"Ok, what do you propose?"

What if, while we were alone in the lift, I confessed my overwhelming desire to have sex with her? What if I informed her that my desire to kiss her lips, neck, breasts, and white hands was irresistible? What if... I had withdrawn my hand and felt already squeezed, crushed, oppressed, and compressed by everything in that city: the faces of people, the tension in the air, and even the restaurant furniture, the chairs, the tables, the transparent wall... I was a complete and utter nobody who lied and exaggerated to feel more significant.

"I want to buy all your pictures."

She gave me a perplexed look.

"All?"

A tempting demon had me saying, "Yes, all."

Incredulousness glowered in her eyes as she said, "I don't know if you realise what you're asking for. You just admitted that you don't have much money."

"Yes, but I can buy the pictures if they are reasonably priced."

"What do you mean by reasonable?"

"Listen, I'm going to make you an offer, and I want you to consider it seriously before responding. I'm not in a rush, so take your time."

She asked me while puffing on her cigarette and biting her bottom lip, "What's your price?"

"Ten thousand dollars."

After some thought, she remarked, "You're an unbelievable chap, Bassam. You pretend to be in a modest condition, but everyone in this area says the contrary. I learned yesterday in passing that you were planning to donate to the ASM, but you either didn't attend their celebration or altered your mind. I offered to sell you a canvass valued at least $20,000 for only $2,000, but you declined because doing so would be dishonest. You've returned with a lowball offer to acquire the lot for

$10,000 now. You have to agree that discrepancies like those are strange. I don't even know what I should think!"

"Nothing wicked, please, my dear Janet. I mean no harm by making this offer. I loved the paintings and would gladly pay a hefty premium to own them. I apologise if I offended you, Janet, or gave the impression that Robert's work is only worth that much. Of course not; I know full well its priceless value. Do not misinterpret my intent. Please disregard my proposal if you find it unappealing."

"I wouldn't call it unappealing, but it is indeed peculiar. Instead, you can acquire two or three canvasses for that money, maybe even more, but you can't have the whole lot, Bassam. Get it?"

I couldn't shake the impression that we were negotiating for something else.

"I don't need one or two, Janet. I'm looking to buy the complete set. If not, I won't be satisfied."

"Don't behave like a petulant child. Happiness is a mental state, not a place to arrive at. You must learn to make concessions to prosper in life. Also, consider the cost involved in creating these paintings, revealing your lack of realism."

The next second, she was fumbling around for her bag.

"It's either all or nothing," I yelled angrily.

She rolled a cigarette and lit it. She seemed a little disturbed and annoyed. After we had eaten silently for a while, she finally looked up and apologised for her remarks.

"Forget it"

"May I ask you a question, albeit an indiscreet one?"

" Go on, Janet. Just blurt out whatever's on your mind."

"Have you purchased a painting before?"

"Never."

"That's exactly what I was thinking. Why the sudden interest in art, then?"

Surprised, I knew I couldn't give her the whole truth. But what exactly is the truth? My platonic love with her?

"I'm not sure, but I'll be satisfied with the collection regardless."

"Most definitely. If we accept your offer, what are you planning to do with all those images? Will you make a profit by reselling them?"

"Oh no. You are just wrong, sweetie. You assume I want to make money from our interaction, but I have something entirely different in mind. You have probably concluded that I am taking advantage of you because of the details you have revealed about your current predicament... However, this is not correct. Men have other interests besides making a buck. Yes, Janet, we also hold to moral principles. I'd argue that the latter are far more potent, compelling, and alluring. Freedom, justice, dignity, and love... are more than words, my lovely lady."

She looked at me with piercing blue eyes, pondered absently for a few seconds, and then said, "Don't expect a miracle to happen, but If you'd like two or three pictures, I'll discuss it with Robert and let you know the outcome." Please tell me the room number.

"Sixth floor, room 356."

We got up and signed the bill. Afterwards, I escorted her back to the lobby. Later, we said our goodbyes.

I called out " Janet" as she was walking towards the lift.

She turned her head.

"Yes?"

"The complete set!"

"You fool!" she shook her head.

***

I went to the front desk and asked the receptionist whether my car was sold. The reply was negative. After thanking him, I collected the newspapers instead of heading straight to the bank. Since their 'Ouja location is no longer operational, I had to let them know I am still available to work in the Capital. I have better things to do than sit around the hotel doing nothing. Hassan promised me an office at the Sheraton, but I can't wait for him to make the necessary arrangements with the management. What if, after I signed the contract, he suddenly decided that I was no longer helpful to him? I need to be cautious. I could still hear Abdullah Zahir's remarks in my head. He predicted that Hassan and his boss would be among those affected by an impending reorganisation and would thus be replaced. Is this the true motivation for their covert actions? Is it a guess, or do they know? If they don't pay the British company, which they must have paid long ago, and instead keep all that cash for themselves, they may quickly leave the country at the first indication of danger. And if I could return to work at the bank without drawing suspicion, I wouldn't want to throw away fifteen years of experience for nothing. Ultimately, I wasn't too concerned that Zerga hadn't found a new master quite yet. My dear veteran automobile would be extremely helpful on the hectic streets of the Capital.

After picking up my paper at a shop, I left from the hotel's front door. I was striding across the parking lot when I heard my name. Then I turned to see the chauffeur panting after me, baffled, and saying, "Mr Bassam, I was just waiting for you in the lobby. I'm sorry I didn't notice you left until I asked."

I'd entirely forgotten about him, and now that he was around, I didn't know what to do with him. I didn't want him to report all of my movements, which he would if I let him drive me to the bank. I told him, "There's no harm; you may go have a drink and put it on my bill, Khemis. I'll give you a ring if I need your help."

"I am here to help you, sir. But I'll have to drive you if you want to go out. "The orders are clear.

"All right, now go and have a drink, Khemis."

"I'll be waiting right here, sir. You may require my help... I appreciate the drink as well. I'll have it after the service."

What the devil!... Khemis, I realised, was not just a driver but one of Hassan's guys whose primary duty was to keep an eye on me. I had no choice except to dump my cards on the table openly.

"Hold on a second, Khemis. I will get in my car and drive it to the repair shop by myself because it's broken down, and you're of no help right now. That's why I suggested you go and get a drink."

After silence, he stroked his chin with his long, dark fingers and said, "I'll drive it for you, sir. I can recommend a decent maintenance garage near the hotel but don't even think of asking me to leave you alone. If I do that, I'll be fired. Sadly, sir, I have a family. There are seven mouths to feed."

"Well, well, don't worry. Don't worry, I won't wreck your life, but don't bother me either."

"Sir, there are already seven of them here, and another one is on the way."

"Really? Well done, Khemis! Yes, but how do you do it? I guess I'm trying to say how you balance the books. Do you work in the used radio cassette market at all? Are you interested in other people's automobiles so that you might... Ahem... give them away at the Friday Market?"

Khemis could not understand my reference to the 'Ouja police officer who used to steal radio cassettes from stationed cars under his guardianship and sell them on the black market.

"If you are referring to my work during the holidays, I am well forced to do it because I am paid the double of what I actually gain," he said, "but I don't quite understand you, sir."

"How much are you earning if I am not indiscreet?"

"Certainly not, sir; it's no secret. There are just 650 of them."

"Six hundred fifty?" Incredulous, I repeated.

"Yes, sir, but it's barely enough for seven mouths... and..."

"Well, I know Khemis, I know. The eighth is on the way."

But astonishment overcame me in a big way. I was taken aback to learn that despite earning more than I could ever have in my banking career, the chauffeur of the Ministry of the Interior expressed feelings of underpayment. What would he say if I told him the real wage of a bank clerk? But he couldn't do his job as Interior 'chauffeur' very well if he didn't know it. He probably knows that some university professors in our country make less money than security officers. Some of our most illustrious academics, I'm sure, would rather not waste their talents on books and pupils and instead work for the country's most significant government agency. Some scholars, it seems, dream of becoming cops or even super-cops.

To save my face, I said, "It's a real misery, a shame; it's not worthy of the prestigious Ministry of the Interior!" How can you control people with only 650 per month? Yes, I know you're only a driver, Khemis; you don't actually cudgel, hit, kick, torture and perform all the legal work. But aren't you paid to drive those who serve the government? You may eventually drive state guests and other collaborators to the Ministry, and it's all fine! This is not an excuse to treat you with such contempt. What the hell? A driver is important, even at the Ministry of Interior! He could be more significant than a bank teller. What exactly am I saying? God! Please forgive me! A driver is, in fact, more vital than a banker. How about six hundred fifty? It is simply intolerable. In your shoes, I would complain, organise a strike, or perhaps a street protest. You cannot feel secure with such miserable pay, even if you work for the Director of Security himself. Khemis, do you feel safe?"

He looked at me, "lost in the translation"! He'd already started gnawing his fingernails and rolling his eyes.

"Are you serious, sir?" I am secure, but it is insufficient. I spend my entire salary every month in the first two weeks and then begin borrowing. Furthermore, there is no trade union for state agents, sir. We have only Allah to complain to."

"Allah is forgiving and generous, Khemis. I'll speak with Hassan about you and your compensation. I'll request that it be increased to 700. Is it okay?"

"Oh, sir, I am grateful to you. However, I don't want to bother you with my problems."

"There is no botheration whatsoever. Your boss is a good friend of mine. This is a promise. Now go have a drink in my honour."

He took his time getting ready to leave. I looked down at my watch, which was nowhere to be seen around my wrist. I'd taken it off before showering and had forgotten it in my room. So I inquired of Khemis, "What time is it?"

"It's ten past ten, sir."

I noticed he was wearing a beautiful watch bracelet around his wrist. It was a costly vagary for a chauffeur. I had no doubt that the watch was worth his salary if it was confirmed that he was paid 650 dinars monthly. He could have been lying.

"Khemis, show me your watch." This is a lovely item; where did you obtain it?"

He showed me his wrist where his shining watch was, basking in the sunlight.

"It's an old watch, sir, that I inherited from my father. Nothing like it can be found currently. It's as accurate as Big Ben."

"Really? How much do you want for it?"

"How much for what, sir?"

"I'm asking about the price of the watch because I want to buy it."

Surprised, he exclaimed, "But I don't intend to sell it, sir."

I took my wallet out and opened it. It didn't have much cash. "This is for the drink, Khemis," I said as I pushed some torn banknotes into his pocket. "Tell me your price, and I'll give you a cheque."

He mumbled something in response, staring blearily at the chequebook in my hand. He was obviously apprehensive.

"What's the big deal? Fifty dinars aren't enough? Is it okay if I make you climb to the thousand? Now, what's your price?"

He ploughed his hair with his fingers.

"It isn't easy, sir. However, thank you very much. I am grateful."

He opened the bracelet, removed it, and handed it to me.

"It's heavy," I commented after weighing the watch. "How much is it?"

"It's made of gold and silver, sir. It's extremely expensive and rare. But for you, it's a gift. Please accept it, Sir.

"Thank you so much, Khemis. Because I don't want to insult you by rejecting your present, I'll take it. Now, if I can't keep my promise, I'll give it back to you; after all, I never accept bribes. It's one of my principles."

I wrapped the watch around my wrist and dashed across the parking lot. Khemis stood outside the hotel's gate while I drove past him and waved. What did he make of it? Instead of letting him drive me, I trapped him. That was a successful deal in which I lost nothing. If I continue on this path, which I intend to do, I will be the most powerful businessman in the country very soon, and it is not unlikely that I will surpass even Hassan. The next time I am compelled to purchase helicopters for the State, I shall include the following conditions: it is now 90% for me and 10% for my associates.

For now, Hassan has lost: his spy has been neutralised as long as I hold his valuable watch. Indeed, I have no intention of intervening on his behalf because I know I will be severely disciplined if I do. Anyway, his pay is perfectly adequate; I even envied him, but he is greedy and his greed cost him his father's valuable bequest. If this lesson does not teach him anything, I will strip him naked and return him to his boss bare as a worm.

***

Fifteen minutes later, I was going through the bank's grand marble corridor and up to the first floor to meet Mr Khalil, the head of the Human Resources department. I hoped he would remember me from the two or three times we had met at the tedious conferences I had to attend in the Capital with my coworkers from the 'Ouja branch.

I gently knocked on the door and heard a woman's voice. After a few seconds, I banged once more. The voice was still talking, but nobody responded. I hesitated, knocked twice, but didn't bother waiting for a response before turning the knob and poking my head inside. The secretary was on the phone and gave me a stern look before asking, "What the hell do you want? Can't we get five minutes of peace in this brothel?"

"Brothel? But I thought I was at the bank, sister—my bank!"

"I'm not your sister. Clear the way."

Her hand was on the phone's receiver, so I knew her final comment was meant for me.

"Is this not Mr. Khalil's office?"

She pretended not to hear me.

"Who the heck are you?"

"I'm sorry Ma'am, is it Mr. Khalil's office?" I insisted.

She ignored me and went on with her mindless prattle:

"Sweetheart, it was such a blast, and we truly missed you. Guess who became the centre of attention at the party!... haha... Really, who spilled the beans?... You'd be shocked to know how inebriated she was... Indeed, I've never seen her like that before... She was completely out of it... She got so carried away that she shed all her garments, danced atop the table, and even planted her foot in someone's cake... And haha... He, quite intriguingly, held her foot and started to lick it."

I gently pushed the door open and approached her desk leisurely. As I neared, she appeared alarmed; ceasing her conversation, she placed her hand on the phone's receiver and glared disdainfully at me.

"Who the hell are you? What do you want?"

"I've been standing here for the past five minutes, Ma'am. It seems you chose to ignore me. I need to confirm, is this Mr. Khalil's office? Yes or not."

She was visibly annoyed.

"I told you to clear out."

"I'm not your butler, Ma'am, but your colleague from 'Ouja Bank. My name is Bassam Bourasin."

" Ok. I've heard you. Did you get an appointment?"

"I didn't, but I believe he'll make time for me."

" Impossible. He won't see you without an appointment. Mr. Khalil has a packed schedule, and I'm quite busy as well. Kindly, go home and come back when you got an appointment."

"I really can't delay, Ma'am. Kindly let him know that Mr. Bourasin wishes to speak with him, or I'll have to force my way."

She looked utterly shocked. However, realising my determination, she pressed the intercom button and relayed:

"Mr. Khalil, there's an individual here who's quite insistent on meeting you immediately... No, sir, he identifies as an employee of 'Ouja... yes, Mr...?"

"Bassam Bourasin," I interjected.

She echoed my name. After a momentary pause, she eyed me with a mixture of contempt and anxiety and said:

"OK. Mr. Khalil will see you in a minute."

My audacity was making a mark. In a different scenario, I might have patiently stood outside, letting the secretary indulge in her frivolous phone chat before gracing me with her attention. Only then, and after scheduling an appointment days later, would she consider notifying her superior of my presence. Acquiring that appointment would involve tiresome negotiation, given the immense workload of HR. "This isn't just 'Ouja', it's the CAPITAL, for heaven's sake! You can't just barge in, especially not without prior notice, expecting a warm welcome even as an employee. This institution is a bank, not some rowdy establishment! Don't you understand?" I was well aware of it. That's why, until now, I hadn't dared to set foot in the main office. The right moment had to come.

I comforted myself with modest aspirations for nearly a decade and a half. I'd daydream about visiting the headquarters once I was elevated to deputy director or perhaps the manager of 'Ouja Bank. While I had no intention of challenging Mr Aroussi, who had consistently earned my loyalty, I, too, harboured dreams. In these visions, there was room for both his advancement and mine. Mr. Aroussi's fall from grace deeply saddened me. I felt sorry for him more than for myself because I knew that his disgrace would preclude or delay my promotion if it didn't accelerate my degradation and turn me into a tawdry victim of the Administration, which it ineluctably did when I was incarcerated a few days after his arrest. True, I was not expecting the Islamist counter-coup, nor that a casual acquaintance from my jail days would be elevated to a high position and thus propose to make me a happier man - with two hundred thousand dollars on the table and a promised stay in paradise with an Houry named Sophia!

With these exhilarating thoughts playing like a festive tune in my mind, it's not surprising that I confidently strode into the head office as if I'd made a grand entrance from my private helicopter. It was the first time I genuinely felt empowered, and ready to converse with a higher-up as an equal. I might've even requested to meet the Chairman, but that wasn't the need of the hour.

Mr. Khalil seemed taken aback by my unexpected appearance. Although he greeted me politely, he quickly made it clear he wasn't interested in revisiting the past — that's how he perceived my awkward reference to our previous encounter with Mr. Aroussi.

"Mr. Bassam, on a personal note, I bear no grudge against him. However, his reputation here has soured. Given his actions, he's now viewed as a traitor, and in my opinion, he's earned any consequences. But let's stay on track, how may I assist you today?"

The individual in front of me starkly contrasted with the friendly Mr. Khalil I remembered, who once enjoyed light moments during tedious banking presentations. Instead, I now saw a more reserved figure, seemingly shielded by his role as a senior bank official. His gaze, filtered through thick spectacles over his grey eyes, was cautious, and he seemed almost protective in his cushioned chair.

"I wanted to let you know that I'm prepared to continue my role."

"A letter would have been more appropriate, Mr. Bassam.

However, since you're here, I regret to inform you that there's still no verdict regarding our 'Ouja' branch."

"I'm aware, sir. I realise the 'Ouja' branch isn't reopening soon, especially given the repairs needed. The destruction I witnessed was devastating... A tragedy of immense scale. I tragically lost my mother and fiancée in the chaos."

"I'm deeply sorry to hear that. But, continuing..."

"Yet, I believe you know, sir, that the bank's staff can't simply wait for the renovations. I've heard some of my colleagues have been reassigned to the main office, and for your information, I've dedicated fifteen years of service to this institution."

Mr Khalil cleared his voice and said:

"Mr Bassam, things aren't quite as you perceive. In fact, many of your colleagues have been relocated to other branches of the bank, and only a handful remain here. All these movements are temporary. As for your situation, it's a bit complicated. You've been absent for months, and there isn't any directive about your return."

I interjected:

"Khalil, after years of dedication, you can't just dismiss someone without justification, right?"

He replied:

"No one said you're dismissed. However, should that decision be made, it won't be by me but the higher-ups. If they choose to recognise your services and let you go, my role would be to implement that. Your situation is tricky because, despite being one of our top employees, you were imprisoned with Mr Aroussi, who's now facing serious allegations."

"I've no connections with him," I countered. "If I weren't innocent, I wouldn't be standing here."

Khalil nodded.

"I understand, but you've been missing for several months, not just a few days. The bank needs clarity, especially with our reputation at stake. I'm sorry, but you must see how complex this is."

"So, what's the next step? An investigation?"

He sighed.

"Most likely. And Mr Bassam, even if your innocence is established, the process might drag on due to bureaucratic hurdles."

"You're not suggesting I remain unemployed in the interim? You could reinstate me while the inquiry is ongoing," I proposed.

He contemplated.

"What if the investigation doesn't favour your reinstatement?"

"Why wouldn't it? I was released without trial since they knew I was innocent."

"The police may believe so, but the bank has its considerations. Beyond your sudden arrest and subsequent release, they might delve into your personal life, associations, and more. They could exonerate you or let you go with due compensation. I genuinely wish you well, but my influence is limited. I can urge them to expedite, but that's about it."

Feeling cornered, I said:

"If the higher-ups decide on this course, so be it. But I won't be sidelined easily. I've been loyal to this bank for 15 years and have rights, primarily to challenge decisions that disregard my contributions. If you aim to oust me due to my arrest, tread carefully. Legal counsel is still available in this country."

"Bassam, you need to understand your position within the bank. It would be wise for you to remain silent and patiently wait for the administration's decision. Even if the bank terminates your employment, they will likely offer you a fair severance. Why risk your reputation by behaving irrationally? It's not a wise move."

"I'm not being irrational, sir. I'm standing up for my worker's rights. They deserve respect."

"You should recognise that you're not the only one in this predicament. We're facing staff cuts, even here in the Capital. The new regime isn't supportive of our banking methods. We're currently in talks with them, and the bank's future hangs in the balance."

"I might have connections that could help, Mr. Khalil. If you keep me in the right position, I can reach out to influential government figures."

He laughed sarcastically, "It's amusing to think that a clerk like you could assist in our high-level negotiations."

"I'm offering more than just connections. I want a chance to show my commitment to this bank. Let me handle the repairs at the 'Ouja office. If you hire an external company, it'll cost the bank millions. I'll do it for half the price. I have a deep attachment to the 'Ouja branch. I know you have the influence to make this happen, Mr. Khalil."

He looked genuinely surprised, his face momentarily contorting in confusion before settling into an uneasy smile. "Is this a jest?"

"No, Mr. Khalil. I'd hate to see someone else get the contract."

He appeared stunned.

"I assumed you were only here to continue as a clerk."

"My position as a clerk doesn't prevent me from having business aspirations. They're not mutually exclusive."

"There's a clear distinction between a clerk and a business-man. It's impossible to be both."

"Why not? My name, Bourasin, means 'double-headed.' Fifteen years ago, when I joined the bank, no one had issues with my name. Did you forget?"

"That's just a name, Mr. Bourasin. We couldn't change that. My shock isn't about the fact but your audacity." He hesitated, then said, "Still, I see where you're coming from."

"I'm pleased you understand."

"I heard about your mother's tragic demise. My deepest sympathies, Mr Bassam. Kindly excuse my absent-mindedness; I've been swamped with work lately."

As I readied to leave, I said:

"I don't wish to impose further on your valuable time, sir."

However, he responded energetically:

"Wait, wait! You're not causing any inconvenience, Mr Bassam. Sit down, please, and pardon my oversight. How thoughtless of me not to offer you a beverage. What can I get you – coffee, tea, or something else?"

I couldn't help but note his abrupt change in demeanour.

"It's quite alright, Mr Khalil. Your gesture is appreciated, but..."

He cut me off, saying:

"Actually, it's my error. I overlooked basic courtesy. As my guest – or rather, the bank's guest – not just an employee, you should have something to drink." He pressed a buzzer on his desk, instructing, "Kindly get us some refreshments. Mr Bourasin, what would you like?"

Still surprised but willing to engage, I replied:

"Just a coffee for me."

"Would you like milk in it?"

"No, just black, thank you."

"Very well, two black coffees, please, Miss. And while you're at it, please retrieve Mr Bassam Bourasin's file. I'd like to check if his salary for the past six months has been processed correctly."

***

When I left the bank about twenty minutes later, I had secured three commitments: My previously withheld six-month salary would soon be available in my head office account. A new role in the external transactions department awaited me, starting October 1st. Furthermore, I was allowed to oversee the repairs of our 'Ouja premises. In return, a small commission would go to Mr Khalil, but only if he secured my repair contract. He initially hoped for a fifty per cent cut, but I managed to negotiate it down to twenty-five per cent. We decided to keep in touch to finalise the contract details. I informed him of my stay at the Sheraton, which seemed to shock him, given the sudden turn in my fortunes. He assumed I had come into a substantial inheritance from my late mother and was exploring potential investments. I did not correct his misconception, seeing no need to reveal all my cards. However, his curiosity about the size of my inheritance was evident, as he kept suggesting various investment opportunities. It was clear he wanted a sense of the scale of my wealth. When I casually mentioned a figure of 'two hundred million dollars,' he nearly choked on his hot coffee, breaking into a fit of coughing that only subsided after he downed half a bottle of water. Composing himself, he declared:

"Kudos, Mr Bourasin! Undoubtedly, you're our bank's most esteemed employee, and I'll ensure the bank capitalises on your newfound prosperity."

Three

Returning to the hotel, I mulled over my discussion with Mr. Khalil. His friendship seemed full of potential, grounded on shared interests. I mused about how splendid it'd be if everyone displayed such practicality, warmth, and service-oriented nature. If only life were that simple! Khalil's character intrigued me - was he innocent or driven by greed? Perhaps both. I wondered if I'd act similarly in his shoes.

Life then felt straightforward, almost inviting, a moment of pure joy. Navigating the bustling lanes of the Capital brought back memories. With its seductive yet oppressive nature, the city was a place I'd consciously avoided for a good portion of my career. Those cluttered streets, dense with glass and concrete buildings, always made me feel lost, insignificant, and overwhelmed. It often seemed as if the metropolis was a monstrous entity waiting to consume the unworldly villager in me. It was the allure of its pleasures I had to resist lest I get sucked into its vibrant vortex. Each visit was marked by my apprehensions, camouflaged by an air of aloofness and false pride.

Many peers found solace in the city's bars, nightclubs, and other entertainment venues. While the idea of a drink, a gamble, or a fleeting romance did allure me, I never truly gave in – a possible result of my puritanical beliefs. Reflecting on my past, especially my time in jail, losing my loved ones, and dealing with the Security Director, I wonder if I've changed. Am I still the man I once knew? The uncharacteristic encounter with Mrs Waterbird in the elevator further deepens this quandary. Such audacious thoughts were alien to me just a while back when I led a regular life working at 'Ouja Bank.

Clearly, I was in love because of an imagined encounter with Janet Waterbird in the Sheraton's lift. It felt like I had Janet in every possible way except physically. My passion was so intense that it mentally consumed me. Even now, I'm caught in this emotional web with her, and it seems we both played a part in turning a potential romance into mere platonic affection. Sometimes, I wonder whether I'm not chasing illusions. My perceptions have been so skewed that I've reduced a real lady with beauty like none other into just a mental image - much like the elusive Jennia of Haj Mukhtar. These could be lingering old habits that I thought were long gone. I once believed that physical intimacy wasn't necessary to understand love, a notion I now see as misguided. While I was committed to Dalila, I upheld a chaste mindset, except for visiting the whorehouse. But with her gone, I feel no need to hold onto that ideology. Who will celebrate my successes with me as I navigate life's waters? Of my acquaintances and kin, no one remains to share in the joy of my personal journeys in a city that has often been harsh and frustrating. Only Zerga, my loyal car, remains with me, like a relic from a world of oblivion. Alas, she might make odd sounds, but she can't communicate in clear words.

Driving with these thoughts, I slowed down upon seeing

the red light at a crossroad. Suddenly, I thought I heard a mysterious and familiar voice from within the car: "Congratulations! You're making great strides."

Instinctively, I responded, "Thanks, Zerga. I feel your happiness for me. I wouldn't trade you for all the riches in the world."

"I know you wouldn't betray me," said the enigmatic voice, "that's why I'm here."

Almost instinctively, I retorted, "Of course."

Only at that moment did I realise my folly. I was conversing with a voice I attributed to Zerga, despite knowing cars can't talk. Shocked and terrified, I glanced back. A woman, draped in a dark cloak that covered her head, peered at me with one eye - the other concealed behind a black patch. Did she climb into the car when I stopped at the traffic lights or before? Did she mistake it for a cab? Lost in thought and overwhelmed by the city's noise, I hadn't noticed her. But her unexpected presence stirred me, and I couldn't hide my annoyance.

Here's the rewritten content:

"Get out, grandma; this isn't a taxi."

"Don't yell, son of a bitch, I can hear just fine. Keep driving."

For her age, her voice held a distinct roughness and vitality. Moreover, she curses!

"How dare you? If you don't leave immediately, I'll call the cops. Such unacceptable behaviour! It's utterly shocking!"

"Press on, jerk; the signal is green! Don't test my patience."

"I'm not your driver, grand'ma; I've told you..."

"I am not your grand mother, you fucking son of a bitch."

Suddenly, a gun materialised in her grasp, partially concealed by her voluminous sleeve. She aimed it squarely at me, proclaiming:

"See this? Proceed swiftly, before I snap. It's ready to fire, and should you act smart, remember that my finger's pretty jittery over here."

Overwhelmed, my eyes darted to a policeman shaded from the sun by a coffee shop awning. Yet, he appeared oblivious to the drama unfolding in my vehicle. How I hoped he'd approach to inspect any random document or that my car would suddenly malfunction, compelling his attention. I desired a minor collision, but fate ignored my silent pleas. All I experienced were the intense sunbeams hitting my windshield, almost blinding, and the murmured conversations of the coffee shop patrons on the patio, all against a backdrop of urban sounds and the steady purr of surrounding vehicles.

Navigating past the crossroad and making a right, the grating voice of the brusque woman echoed again. There was a familiar bite in her tone, though I couldn't pinpoint where I'd heard it before. But I'm sure I knew that voice as if it was the devil's or angel who haunts me for centuries.

"Where do you think you're headed?" she inquired.

"Returning to my hotel. Where should I drop you?"

"At your hotel," she responded, unperturbed.

"It's the Sheraton. Might be a tad luxurious for your taste... unless, of course, you plan on using your... weapon... as leverage."

"Feeling witty? Fine, I trust you won't let your so-called 'aunt' foot her own bill."

"I've no aunt, and my mother has passed."

"Sympathies, young man. But from this point forward, consider me your aunt. Clear?"

With great indignation, I exclaimed:

"You truly don't get it, grandma. I'm just a mere guest at that hotel. I can't even afford my room, let alone have any extra money. How could I possibly pay for you?"

"There's no need for an additional room, my dear nephew. Your room will do for both of us. Just say I'm your aunt here to see a doctor for my arthritis. And don't push me to converse; it might not end well for you. To everyone else, I'm mute and deaf. Clear?"

"I understand, but what's this charade all about? As I said, I'm broke. You're barking up the wrong tree if you plan to rob me. This car I'm driving? We'd be lucky to make it to the hotel without it breaking down."

"Don't act clever, Bassam. It's in your best interest to get me to your room without any issues. I'm armed."

She knew my name, yet I couldn't place the voice that bore a resemblance to hers. The voice wasn't particularly feminine - it was rough, commanding, coarse, and very much male. When she said my name, a possibility crossed my mind, but I immediately brushed it off as implausible. On impulse, I slammed the brakes, causing the car to screech to a halt.

"Damn you, son of bitch! Do you intend to kill me?"

The sudden stop jolted her. She fell forward, grabbing at the seat cushion. As she pulled back, she inadvertently revealed her face. I turned and, in sheer disbelief, blurted out:

"Hamda?! This is unbelievable!

"Yes, it's me, Hamda. Satisfied now?"

I was stunned, struggling to comprehend. Before me was Hamda La'war, dressed in women's clothing.

"I assumed you were down south."

He regained his composure, smirking in response:

"It's evident I'm not in the fucking south."

"So, they're still on your tail? That explains the disguise. I'm sorry, but this isn't the right time for your theatrics. There was no need to hide your true self; you're just making a spectacle."

His temper flared.

"Get moving! You're clueless."

He veiled his face once more. It was then I noticed his missing moustache. It used to add character, but without it, he looked pitiful, reminiscent of a scalded rat.

We resumed our journey, navigating a narrow lane where vendors vocally peddled their produce from wooden stalls. I had to be extremely cautious to avoid hitting the throngs of pedestrians around them.

"You can't stay hidden in the hotel," I asserted. "They're aware of my identity, thinking I'm a prosperous businessman, and they're monitoring me."

A loud laugh escaped him.

"A businessman? Oh, that's rich!"

His laughter irked me. "Why do you find that so amusing? Seems like you don't take my words seriously."

He snorted, "Young man, I trust no one."

"Perhaps this once you should. I'm being candid... Truly, you..."

But he cut me off swiftly:

"Enough, Bassam! I've known you since you were a little boy. Remember when I took you under my wing? You owe your training, everything, to me. And now you're advising me? Yes, they're after me, but it's temporary. Soon, we'll be back in 'Ouja, ruling this country."

"You're deluding yourself, Mr. Hamda. The Islamists control now, and it'll be a while before their grip loosens. Think of another safe haven. It's not that I won't assist, but they're tailing me too. They've infiltrated the hotel, they'll spot you, and then…"

"They're unaware you have an aunt, aren't they? They won't trouble an elderly woman, especially one who's deaf and mute, just going to visit a doctor. In the meantime, our allies will mobilise."

"Allies? Whom are you referring to?"

"The Americans, boy."

His statement befuddled me. "I'm lost."

He rolled his eyes. "Of course you are. You always were a bit slow. American Embassy staff are out in the city, distributing money to the locals."

"Really? How charitable! Americans have always been so generous. Look at the aid they provide to impoverished nations. It's quite the sum, millions annually."

He scowled, "You naive fool! It's not charity. They're orchestrating a counter-coup, buying loyalties - trade unions, the unemployed, the disgruntled masses. Soon there will be protests, strikes, all starting in the Capital. Anarchy will reign, fires will burn, blood will spill. Once chaos ensues, our forces will strike, pushing the Islamists out."

I gaped at him. "Are you being genuine or pulling my leg?"

His face darkened, "Have I ever joked about such grave matters?"

He had a point, but I countered, "Maybe it's just a baseless rumour. We do have a penchant for gossip."

Hamda bristled, "This is the grim reality, Bassam. I've seen money bags exchanged with union leaders. Soon, all public services will halt, strikes will ensue. The people will rise against the government. Then, supported by this foreign money, our forces will mobilise. We'll target key locations, including the Presidential Palace..."

I gasped, "That's sheer insanity! They'll be annihilated."

"There will be losses, but we're prepared. I'm coordinating our party's forces in 'Ouja."

"But how? The Islamists have taken over 'Ouja. It's swarming with their militias."

"I might not need to go there," he replied cryptically. "In fact, I have a better candidate in mind. When I saw your car at the red light, I knew it was fate. This is your moment, Bassam. Time to show allegiance to the motherland."

"You mean the 'party', right?"

He gave a wry smile, "The party will always be OUR motherland."

"But after the Islamist coup, the dynamics have shifted, Mr. Hamda. The old party isn't what it was. Now there's a new party claiming dominance. And just to be clear, while I am loyal, I stay out of politics. Reporting is one thing. Courting danger is another."

His grip tightened on my shoulder. I glimpsed his furious eye in the rearview. His unexpected return had stolen my happiness, casting a shadow over my life. It felt like I was trapped in a never-ending nightmare mirroring the fate of our beleaguered nation.

His voice was icy, "Are you denying me your assistance?"

"I regret the misunderstanding, Mr. Hamda. While you stand as a beacon for national heroism, I simply wish to safeguard my modest life and daily bread, no more.

His eyes narrowed, a sneer forming on his lips.

"Just a modest life? Bread?" He spat out, the disdain evident in his voice. "Is this a jest to you? When the nation calls out, you choose deafness? It's cowardice, pure and simple. Do you think we won our freedom with such attitudes? We battled not mere rebels but a monstrous empire!"

I took a deep breath, finding the courage to continue.

"Mr. Hamda, my ties to your battles, past or present, are tenuous at best. I was born in what is deemed a liberated country. My education on colonisation came from people like you, who felt it their duty to instill a deep-seated animosity for foreign rulers. I harbor no ill feelings towards the British, the French, or any European nation for that matter. But if nationalism implies despising others, I am no nationalist. The lines blur for me between colonisation and nationalist governance. Both, in my eyes, are flawed systems. The exploitation during colonial times is mirrored in our nationalist rule. Our newfound freedoms have been twisted into shackles. The vibrant dreams of liberty have turned into haunting nightmares. This nation, once sovereign, feels more like a vast estate where we're nothing more than serfs. You sowed the tempest that threatens to swallow this nation. You replaced one tyranny with another. And now, in your regime's downfall, you beckon the Americans? Is this the nationalism you touted? Swapping British rule for American oversight? How do they differ, Mr. Hamda? If you're so fond of foreign influence, why not settle abroad? Can we really be deceived by your outdated nationalistic anthems? You and your ideology are remnants of a bygone era. It seems to me your brand of nationalism stifles genuine ambition and crushes any hope of a truly representative governance. Let me be clear, Mr. Hamda. If I ever aided you, it was out of fear, not belief. My regrets are profound now. I may not favour the new regime, but my disdain for you and your methods far outweighs that. My incarceration, the undue pressures, the likely orchestration of my arrest due to petty disagreements— all point towards you. Mr. Aroussi's surprise at my arrest confirmed my suspicions of your involvement."

The car filled with an oppressive silence, a tangible tension that felt almost suffocating. The hum of the vehicle and the glaring sun outside were the only reminders of reality. The looming structure of the Sheraton in the distance was both a beacon of hope and a symbol of looming dread. Pushing down on the accelerator, a voice broke the stillness.

"You fool, Bassam. You've exposed yourself," Hamda whispered menacingly.

The chilling touch of a gun pressed against my neck suddenly made me fearfully freeze.

***

At a close distance from the hotel's wall, I pulled over the car and looked Hamda directly in the eyes. The tension between us was palpable, but I maintained my composure.

"What's the reason for stopping now?" he demanded.

"Mr. Hamda, you're about to step into a hornet's nest. The hotel is swarming with law enforcement and undercover agents. They'll identify you instantly. There's still a chance for you to escape them. Seize it, or you might live to regret it."

He looked at me, unwavering, and directed his gun at me, remarking:

"With this faithful ally by my side, I fear none. Whatever I've shared, relay it. Anything beyond that is not your concern."

"There's much you're unaware of. I have ties with the Ministry of the Interior. Consider this a heads-up."

I aimed for utmost transparency and honesty, but he countered:

"Old news."

"Perhaps it's not novel information, but the dynamics have shifted. You know that I can't foot the bill for an extended stay at the Sheraton. I'm currently under the patronage of the Ministry, and it goes without saying that I'm under strict observation. Moreover, the Director of National Security might be anticipating my arrival at the hotel as we speak."

He contemplated my words.

"So, you've scaled the ladder quickly... Your treachery might have earned you a spot, but I don't commend you on your quick monkey-like climbing. You deceived us; you deserve nothing more than a gunshot in the head."

"Killing me won't be of any benefit to you. I was about to suggest a possible arrangement..."

"Trading my safety for your life?"

"Either way, it amounts to the same thing for both of us."

"Spill it."

"I'll heed your advice. However, while in my room, you must ensure your actions remain discreet and refrain from meddling in my business."

"How can I trust you won't turn against me?"

"I assure you, Mr. Hamda, you have my absolute word. But if your scheme prevails, ensure my safety and recall that I was on your side when the stakes were high."

"And if things don't go as planned?"

"You should vanish and erase every trace of me from your memory."

"You little opportunistic pig!" he exclaimed with disdain.

"In essence, I'm a reflection of you," I responded, "All of you are apex predators in a constant battle. With every violent act, your insatiable cravings only amplify. The common folk are mere pawns in your grand game, sacrificed for your relentless hunger for dominance, wealth, and control. The distinction between you and your rivals is blurred. You're cut from the same cloth. Your battles make it evident that you are virtually identical, as indistinguishable as two similar contagions. You must remember that I've never posed a threat to you. By the same token, don't anticipate any opposition from me towards your adversaries, who currently hold the reins. Involving myself is futile. If you intend to communicate with your allies at 'Ouja, know that my loyalty has its limits. If your stay extends to two or even three days, I promise discretion. Post that, you're on your own. Regardless of our past interactions, I refuse to be the catalyst for your capture or demise. But if you emerge victorious by chance, remember that it was my intervention that ensured your survival."

***

A short while later, our entrance into the Sheraton was as

striking as anticipated. At the reception, the attendant turned to the enigmatic woman in a black cloak standing beside me and asked:

"Can I assist you, madam? Are you here for a room or to meet someone?"

I quickly responded, "She's with me. This is my Aunt Hamida. She's here to consult a doctor about her arthritis. She'll be staying with me until her appointment is set. She's elderly and, unfortunately both deaf and mute."

The man apologised briefly and suggested, "You'll need an additional room then, sir. We can provide room 357; it's right next to yours. There's just a door separating them, which remains locked. I can hand over the key if you wish to get in touch."

"That'll work," I replied.

While I was filling out the register for my illiterate aunt, he interrupted, "Hold on, sir. Mr. Ali, our manager, mentioned you earlier today. He'd like to meet you, perhaps over a drink if you have a few minutes to spare."

"I'd be happy to see him soon," I said, thinking about the generous donation I had promised his organisation.

"Any other messages for me?" I inquired.

"Yes, a friend of yours called from the Ministry. He mentioned joining you for dinner."

Having only one friend in the Ministry, Hassan, I braced myself for the evening.

"Do you need assistance with your aunt's luggage?"

"There's no need; she's not carrying any luggage and won't be here long."

We then made our way to the lift, my aunt's black cloak

dragging behind her; her presence felt like a weighty chain around my ankle. It dawned on me that our troubles were beginning. If not detected and arrested, the masquerade may drag on for a long time. That deadly complicity reassured me in the same way as living with a dormant predator.

The journey to the sixth floor was uneventful. My main concern was bumping into the Waterbirds; explaining my aunt's sudden appearance would be awful. I was sure Hassan would know about the new development if he asked the front desk. I noticed the driver's absence in the lobby, assuming he was probably at the Cafeteria.

Upon entering my room, Hamda discarded his veil and requested the key to the next room. His face was grotesquely painted, both garish and pitiful. I would have chuckled at his comically swollen face in any other situation. However, my current disposition was far from lighthearted.

"I handed it to you in the lift," I remarked.

He gestured toward the door dividing the two spaces, saying, "Not that key, I mean the adjoining door." I had planned to keep that door locked. The last thing I desired was him barging into my space at any given time, especially while I was penning down my observations on what I already perceived to be the tragic fate of the Islamic Republic, which if I believe Hamda, is born doomed.

"No need for that key," I responded with surprise, "just knock if you require something."

His response was firm, "That's not sufficient. I need that key to ensure you won't deceive me."

Following a tense altercation, I relented. It was clear he distrusted me as much as I did him. He unlocked the intermediary door and went to his quarters, mentioning he'd bathe. In the meantime, I arranged for our meals.

***

As afternoon shadows crept past the clock's hands, positioning themselves at 2 p.m., I was ensconced in a cocoon of dreams, the tether to reality manifested only by the persistent chime of the telephone. Half submerged in slumber, my fingers grasped the cold receiver as I murmured, lost in a delirious haze, "Greetings from 'Ouja Bank…"

An apologetic voice responded, "My apologies, sir. An oversight, it seems." Silence followed. Then, clarity pierced my fog of sleep, revealing the gossamer thread of a dream where I had risen to directorship at 'Ouja Bank'. I resent the phone's cold intrusion, the unseen caller who had torn my dreams asunder. A second call, insistent, forced me from my coveted reprieve. Determination swelled; I would not let this interloper mar my rest.

I answered in a measured tone, only to be greeted by a familiar voice: "Mr. Bassam?"

"Robert?" I exclaimed, the surprise evident.

"How fares the day?"

Our conversation meandered from pleasantries to the proposal I had mentioned to Janet. Shortly, he entered, an enigmatic package tucked beneath his arm. Before our rendezvous, I had taken a swift detour to check on Hamda, finding him in a post-feast repose, evidence of his indulgence strewn around.

Returning, I settled in as Robert sat in the recliner near the expansive window, placing his modest yet mysterious package on the nearby table. His parcel was whispering tales of its contents. With a wistful sigh, he began, "Janet left for shopping. I didn't want her to go out alone. Yet, the solitude she granted was a balm. She's constantly on my tail, and she's a goddamn fucking moralist!"

He spoke of unsettling murmurs in town, of an undercurrent of unrest amongst the youth. His words painted the picture of a city on the brink of tumult, juxtaposed with our serene surroundings.

"I believe we'll need two glasses and some ice," said I. Fortunately, the rooms are better equipped. "I believe I have some ice in the fridge."

"Well, whatever! I'm quite thirsty. Give us some ice."

As I facilitated his request, opening the fridge to retrieve ice, I offered words of reassurance regarding Janet, painting her as a robust woman in a currently tranquil city. Robert, however, cast doubt on the perceived calmness, bringing attention to brewing unrest in the campus area close to our location. He spoke of a significant assembly orchestrated by students, a situation often teetered on the edge of chaos, inducing clashes with law enforcement. He reflected on the personal turmoil experienced due to their son's turbulent phase at a university in England, a time that etched worry deep into their hearts.

In the muted ambience of the room, he unveiled the bottle. I set a pair of glasses on the table, and the symphony of ice cubes danced as they fell into them. Adjacently, I placed an ornate dish carved from white copper, brimming with ice, and confessed:

"I'm unmarried, and it doesn't look like I'll be soon."

With a thoughtful motion, he filled our glasses.

"My condolences. Janet shared the tale of your kin's ordeal. The solitude of one's homeland can be profoundly haunting."

" "Never mind, Robert! These are turbulent times, indeed. Let us raise our glasses to the guardians in blue who vow to protect the good citizens of this country."

"Truth be told, my heart doesn't sing praises for law enforcement, my friend. Given a choice, my allegiance leans towards the youthful zeal of the students."

"Your sentiment doesn't surprise me. Such disobedience, I believe, is the crucible of art!"

With a mischievous glint in his eyes, he lifted his glass, proclaiming:

"Indeed! Here's to the spirited anarchists, challenging the decayed dogma of f the well-thinking! - Cheers!"

A pang of unease struck me.

"Man, don't yell that loudly. Are you going to throw us both in jail?"

Hardly had the words left my mouth when the middle door burst open. Hamda, like a tempest, stormed in, brandishing his revolver, bellowing:

"Raise your hands! Whom do you speak of imprisoning, traitor? And who's this foreign acquaintance you entertain? Believe not that your English conceals your treachery. Hands skyward, now!"

The raw audacity of the intrusion left us paralysed. Our hands soared in surrender, witnessing the gleaming menace of the revolver as Hamda, draped in his sombre shroud, loomed closer.

"You shouldn't be doing this," Hamda remarked critically,

"Isn't that alcohol? In a predominantly Muslim nation? This isn't right. Wait right here, I might just inform the authorities."

Robert's face turned pale, and he trembled visibly. The glass slipped from his grip, splattering across the plush carpet. Even though Hamda spoke in Arabic, the revolver's sight seemed to unnerve Robert more than his words.

"Who is she? Is she okay? Do you know her?" he asked nervously.

"Calm down, Robert. I'll handle this," I said in English. Turning to Hamda, I spoke in Arabic: "Put the weapon away. You're going to cause problems for all of us. If you escalate this, it won't end well for either of us. Remember our arrangement? You promised not to get involved in my affairs."

"I was just joking around," he responded calmly. Stashing the revolver beneath his cloak, he poured himself some of the alcohol, shocking Robert as he downed it. He leaned back and remarked, "It's quite a good drink, comparable to what one might find in an English pub."

Still reeling from the unexpected behaviour, Robert questioned, "What did she say?"

"That's my Aunt Hamida," I explained, causing a surprised look on his face.

After sharing some context, Robert said with concern, "She's drinking alcohol! Does she even understand? And she had a gun! It could have gone off."

"You've put us in an awkward spot," I responded to Hamda, "He's wondering why you, a supposed devout woman, are drinking."

"If you can bend the rules, why can't I? I don't need to justify myself to anyone," Hamda retorted.

"What's she saying now?" Robert asked.

"She's just expressing her desire to have a drink."

Impressed, Robert said, "Please tell her I admire her spirit and open mind. She's quite unique."

As I translated, Robert offered Hamda another drink. Eager to connect, Hamda tried speaking in English: "Me, friend, good."

Robert laughed, charmed by my aunt's attempt, "She's delightful! A real gem."

Hamda smiled, calming his guard down a little more, "I like your drink."

"Just be cautious," I warned Robert, "She might finish the entire bottle."

Standing up, I went to get another glass. Overhearing Hamda and Robert's light-hearted exchange, I couldn't help but chuckle at the unexpected bond forming between the two.

When I returned to the room, glass in hand, I found Hamda already helping himself to the whisky.

"Don't handle that bottle," I reprimanded in Arabic, trying to keep the fun, "Remember you're pretending to be a woman. At least let us have the pleasure of serving you, dear auntie."

Hamda shot back, "Stay calm, Bassam. If you push me again, I'll forget our friendship and things could turn ugly. I'm not here to be bossed around, alright?"

It was clear the alcohol was already clouding Hamda's judgment. Thankfully, Robert couldn't decipher our Arabic exchange. I took a seat, a plan formulating in my mind. The playing field would level if I could discreetly take the revolver from Hamda. It was pivotal for at least one of us to stay clear-headed. An instinct told me danger was lurking, and past experiences had taught me to trust that instinct. Hassan would be visiting later, and I needed to be sharp. Defusing Hamda or silently diverting his attention had become critical.

The intel Hamda provided was monumental. If Americans were truly entangled in such a secretive scheme, loyalty dictated, I inform Hassan. No diplomat, local or foreign, should brazenly meddle in sovereign matters. Swift action might still prevent the worst outcomes. A decision, and fast, was necessary.

I decided to inform Hassan about the potential conspiracy. However, with the uncertainty of his intentions toward me, I wouldn't say a word until the $200,000 cheque was in my hand. Regardless of the outcome between the government and the insurgents, my survival was non-negotiable. Fulfilling my commitment to Mr. Khalil was impossible without the funds. If I backed out, citing financial constraints, my promised position at the bank would likely evaporate. I pondered mortgaging family assets to secure a loan, but the acquired amount might only cover initial expenses. Substantial funds were crucial to completing the necessary work. I needed to tread carefully, ensuring Hassan comprehended the urgency of my financial need. If he saw reason, all would be well. Otherwise, I was under no obligation to part with vital information.

This was a pivotal juncture in my life. Today's decisions would either catapult me to unprecedented heights or plunge me into an abyss. Everything hinged on the unfolding events.

***

Four

Through the balcony, the room was filled with the muffled light of day and the lively hum of the street. Had I left the window open? It felt like we were on display for the entire city, transgressing its norms behind a mere curtain of smoke. Such an odd assembly we were! A British artist seeking refuge from life's monotony and his wife's dominance; a former leader from a fallen regime, hunted by the police, planning a counter-revolution; and then me, caught in a midlife identity crisis, questioning my role - banker, entrepreneur, spy, or historian?

"Your aunt is one of the most fascinating women I've met in an Arab country. Truly. I admire her resilience against societal expectations."

Robert's eyes darted to my untouched drink, "Not drinking? Need more ice?"

"It's fine, Robert. My aunt seems to be drinking for both of us."

"She sure can handle her liquor!"

From across the room, Hamda shot us a glance. "Is she married? What of her husband?"

"If he knew about this, he'd kill her."

"Then he doesn't need to know. Who would tell him?"

As I relayed the conversation to Hamda, he bristled, "Tell him I'm not married, or you'll regret it!" Struggling with English, he clarified, "He bad. Me, no husband..."

Robert, misunderstanding, replied, "So, your husband wouldn't approve? Brave lady."

"She's trying to say her husband was a wastrel, never truly living."

"Ah! So he's deceased?"

"Yes, he's been gone for years. She feels liberated now."

Robert laughed, "You're as eccentric as your aunt!"

"So, about our arrangement, do you accept my terms?"

"To be honest, I could use the money. But parting with all the artwork for that amount isn't viable. These pieces mean a lot to me."

"I respect that, Robert. I wish to understand the essence of your joy through these pieces. I value them, truly. I told Janet I'd pay any sum, but I have my limits."

Robert paused, "The 'essence of my joy'? What do you mean by that?"

"You seem untouched amidst your art, even as the world succumbs to chaos," I began, observing Robert closely. "You appear unperturbed, venturing into a country on the brink of civil war. Your calmness, even amid uncertain sales, is remarkable. It's clear your art is your sanctuary. While I can't create like you, I thought owning these pieces might offer me a fragment of your peace. After witnessing the horrors in 'Ouja, I'm desperate for any reprieve."

Robert took a contemplative drag from his cigarette. From afar, the call to prayer resonated, "Allah Akbar..."

Hamda, swirling the last of his drink, cut in, "You're referring to the 'Ouja massacre?"

I nodded.

"You have no idea who's behind it."

"Many theories are swirling about, some implicating an ex-sub-officer in..."

Hamda's tone held an edge of urgency." In the troops of our president! That's a silly joke. Let me clarify. Insider sources suggest a deeper conspiracy involving the government. They speak of a clandestine flight, filled with professional assassins. Rumours claim Mamduh and Hassan are entwined in this, using Suleiman Mughli, an infamous thug, to mediate their sinister dealings. The goal? Pin the massacre on our troops, misleading the global community. The Americans' support for us now starts to make sense, doesn't it?"

"Sorry! I can't trust your story."

"Shut up! You were locked up while I was out gathering facts. Remember, my connections run deep, even if they've diminished lately."

"We need concrete evidence, not just words."

He raised his voice, interrupting, "We **have** evidence. Days before the tragedy, a plane landed — filled with hired Mafia hitmen. The intermediary? Suleiman Mughli, a notorious Mafioso. Yet, to divert suspicion, they imprisoned him. Those killers left for Europe the day after. Their aim? Pin the massacre on our troops to alienate us from Western powers. Hassan liaised with Mughli in prison, setting the stage for this. Mughli's Italian wife, frequently in Sicily, became a pivotal player. She set things in motion once she got the nod. Mamduh even met her in Rome a week prior, where plans were solidified with a Mafia chieftain."

He leaned in, eyes blazing, "Deny it if you wish, but you'd be ignoring the glaring truth. We might be tainted, but we're no murderers. We have our informants here and abroad. Doesn't the American commitment make more sense now?"

Stunned by Hamda's revelations, I grappled with disbelief. How could someone like Hassan, who had been so kind to me, be involved in such heinous acts? He'd shown me kindness, treated me like family, and offered opportunities beyond my wildest dreams. Why would he, of all people, be responsible for the deaths of my mother and fiancée? My mind struggled to make sense of it.

While I couldn't believe Hassan was involved, Mughli's involvement was more plausible. His reputation for ruthlessness preceded him. Whether he was hired to kill one or three hundred didn't matter to him as long as he was compensated generously. He wielded unparalleled power, even in prison, feared by all, including judges. Reflecting on our interactions, I remembered his fake compassion, comforting gestures, and reassurance. And the way he hugged me in the hotel lobby, knowing he was free, sent a shiver down my spine.

Mughli was the true puppet master, switching allegiances as easily as one would change shirts. One moment, he was catering to the President's vices, and the next, he was aiding the opposition. Such is the power of the Mafia in this tumultuous landscape.

The truth dawned on me: it wasn't the military but the Mafia that ruled this country. While Mughli's role was expected, given his nefarious reputation, Hassan's potential involvement was what truly rattled me. I'd already heard whispers about the Afghan group's participation and criminal connections. But Hassan? The intellectual with a heart of gold? The thought that he might hide a monster behind his amicable facade was almost unbearable.

His knowledge of my identity before our introduction intensified my confusion. If he played a part in the tragedy, why approach me with offers no one in my position could decline? Was it a bout of guilt, a realisation that his ambition led him astray? Can conscience strike someone capable of orchestrating mass murder? Such an individual would be less of a man and more of an emotionless machine, an automaton fueled by malicious intent. Recollections of Hassan showed no indication of this hidden malevolence. His intentions always seemed genuine. Even when he withheld the money, arguing I'd squander it, I saw it as a protective gesture. As it stands, I owe my improved circumstances to him, right down to the shirt on my back. And the prospect of marrying his sister? It might even be discussed tonight when he comes over.

Certainly, Hassan seemed determined to solidify our bond, perhaps even through familial ties. At first, I assumed my exaggerated claims of wealth swayed him, but it became evident he had a hidden agenda. He recognised my bluff, but instead of reacting with resentment, he offered me a room at the Sheraton, which was a deal that, albeit shady, promised the very fortune I had falsely claimed. We aren't equal in this venture; I'm the vulnerable one. If the scheme falls apart, he and his boss can easily distance themselves, painting me as the sole deceiver. My past sins would conveniently resurface, positioning me as the perfect scapegoat.

I recognised the danger but felt trapped. Rejecting his offer risked not just the loss of newfound privileges but potential imprisonment with legitimate proof of my past crimes. I'd be labelled a traitor, a rat deserving of the harshest punishment. Execution, perhaps, or life in prison. My guilt is undeniable. No excuses, not coercion or blackmail, could forgive my past actions. Choosing a righteous path might have meant hardship, alienation, and the ire of Hamda and his followers, but at least I would've retained my integrity and freedom. Sadly, the same frailty that made me a pawn in Hamda's games drove me into Hassan's intricate web. Afraid of the fallout from past mistakes and drawn by the allure of power, I willingly ensnared myself.

There was no overt coercion, blatant manipulation, or efforts to corner me. Every interaction with Hassan was marked by civility and subtlety. His suggestions were just that – those designed to present me with the best possible solutions. Rather than threatening me with a binding agreement that could imprison me for life if exposed as a fraud, Hassan extended an unexpected lifeline. He offered solace for the loss of my fiancée by suggesting a union with another - his very own sister, Sophia. By doing so, I can't solely blame him for any ill intent without turning that blame inward. If he had a hand in the tragic fate of my loved ones, it was likely a task commissioned by the State, a necessary act for some perceived greater good. He offered me the chance to marry someone precious to him to assuage any potential guilt and balance the scales. In his eyes, it was a gesture that would set things right. Hassan lifted me from the depths of my despair and propelled me to heights I could never have imagined in such a short time. How could I vilify someone who played such a pivotal role in my life? Even if he was somehow connected to the tragedy, it wasn't a targeted attack against my family; they were simply casualties of fate. Perhaps it was just destiny: Mektub!

Within the innermost chambers of my soul, I grappled with the overwhelming weight of equivocation. I stood at a precipice, unable or perhaps unwilling, to confront the starkness of reality. In reflective moments, glimpses of my past were marred by the spectre of subservience, of a life held in the shackles of political servility. Yet, when I dared to cast my thoughts forward, an alternate vision formed — of wedded bliss with Sophia, a life ensconced in luxury, with the world bowing to my newfound status as a man of means. Years hence, memories of 'Ouja's tragedy might fade, becoming mere spectres at the periphery of my consciousness, easily overshadowed by Sophia's radiant smile. Was it worth jeopardising my newfound ascent for abstract principles? Rejecting Hassan's overtures wouldn't breathe life back into the deceased. Instead, I'd find myself returning to life's abyss from whence I emerged. To even utter Hamda's revelations before Hassan would be to tread on dangerous grounds, for power, once attained, is loath to be questioned, mainly when allegations of unspeakable crimes are in the offing. I felt ensnared in a moral quandary, where the choice lay between aligning with the man responsible for my kin's demise in exchange for social elevation and risking all to confront him with a bitter truth. The pull of both paths was equally visceral.

Hamda's account, previously shrouded in scepticism, began to ring with an uncanny truth. I endeavoured to seek solace in doubt, praying his words were woven from falsehood. However, each version of the 'Ouja tale I had encountered paled compared to the intricacy and darkness of Hamda's. Despite his notorious history of deceit, the situation begged me to accord his narrative some credence. My observations cemented this inkling. Hassan spoke volumes of clandestine intentions in the shadowed recesses of the hotel, sharing surreptitious exchanges with Suleiman Mughli. They vanished, reinforcing my belief that their secretive rendezvous bore dark implications.

***

Suleiman had blundered when he leaked to me his appointment with Hassan, and when he perceived his blunder, it was too late. That is why he remained cautiously confined to silence for a moment afterwards. He was rather in a sulky mood as if he were already regretting what he had told me. When I saw Hassan, he did not mention that he was in the hotel the day before our meeting in the Ministry, and I did not dare ask him. What were they meeting secretly for? Indeed, the affairs of the state should not be discussed unless the latter has something to do with the Mafia. I knew the Mughli had helped the Afghan with guns a few months before the Islamist Coup. If both were in prison for some time, it was not unlikely that they would have kept in touch with each other, although they would have been quite discreet, for I noticed nothing before I heard the story of their former cooperation. The point is when exactly Hassan entered the picture. And since I later knew that the Afghan was his rival, I wondered whether the Mafios ignored it. As he had helped the Afghan and, before him, the Scoundrel President, he might as well deal with Hassan and his boss. The more I thought of Hamda's story, the more I found it entirely plausible, and the more I felt myself impotent and miserable.

Furthermore, I knew that Hamda was well-connected. The men of the ancient regime are likely gathering intelligence about the new masters of the country. In such a short period since they took over, the Islamists could not have possibly purged the whole country and cleared away the sympathizers of the secular regime. Some spies are likely undetected in the airport or even at the Ministry of the Interior. Hamda heard the rumour from these spies about the gang of mafiosos landing at the airport like a group of innocent tourists. They perhaps did not attract attention at once, but they were noticed since they had to board the same plane a few days later. The fact that the Minister had been spotted with Suleiman's wife in Italy a little time earlier was to be linked to the group of Italian tourists. They were perhaps not all Italians, but they were all the same since they had arrived on the same plane from the same place. Why a Minister of the Interior should have to meet the wife of a notorious mafioso? Certainly not to lull her about her convicted husband! And where? In Rome, because in Sicilia, there was not the slightest chance that their meeting would remain unnoticed. Rome is a great capital; nobody would care who our Minister was chatting to in any place they chose for the meeting! Nobody but our compatriots, and there are a lot of them living out there, either because they fled the country doomed by coups and counter-coups or because they are long-standing exiles. Some of those chaps would have noticed the bizarre meeting of an Islamist Minister with the mafioso's wife. They had perhaps followed them and reported their movements to their friends or relatives inside the country.

Then, when the massacre of 'Ouja was publicly known, the linkage with the visit to Rome and the group of particularly odd tourists became inevitable. Particularly odd because a gang of Mafiosi, despite all the efforts to conceal their true identity, would unlikely pass unnoticed at the airport, at the hotel, or in any place they would go to. For though those men had perhaps the bashful faces of everybody, sooner or later, their behaviour would betray them. Man is a creature of habit, and I wonder how a Mafiosi gang would behave in our country differently from how it is accustomed to. Even a word uttered randomly, a gesture or a mere glance, would suffice to raise doubts and questions about them. I know my compatriots; their curiosity, confining most often to brash indiscretion, is legendary. They would not fail to plague the Mafiosi and to accost them, as they used to do with ordinary tourists, either to chat or to make some advantageous bargain such as selling traditional goods or exchanging currency, etc... If they did, it is unlikely that they received the accustomed response of the bored ordinary tourist. As they are not wholly idiots, they would wonder about the mystery of that group of tourists with sinister faces, behaving as if they were invited to some funerals. Of course, there is the civil war in the south, and the tourists are no longer eager to visit our country, but those who do are generally kind and courteous. They would cope with the natives and display some sympathy towards them. I do not imagine that the Mafiosi were able to do so. It is merely not their game! I do not say they are unsociable; I know that many of them may be pretty friendly and even affable, perhaps had they left wives and children waiting for them in the country. After all, they are like everybody... But coming over here with the deliberate thought that they are going to slaughter men, women, and children and going back home after that dirty job to meet their wives and kids as if they are returning from an innocuous excursion would leave on their faces the indelible marks of the killing. No eye would miss such a mark. Oh, naturally, because they are used to kill, they are also used to mask the tracks of their crimes. They would display featureless and stone-like faces. I heard of mercenaries fighting, killing, and rampaging for money's sake, and thus supporting revolutions and great causes. It might not have been different, except that there is no cause to fight for in this precise case but merely a sordid slaughter to achieve.

I lit another cigarette and emptied my glass. The taste of whisky in my mouth had become sour, and disgust over-whelmed me again. I looked around and did not understand why we were gathering in that room or the meaning of our meeting.

Absorbed in my thoughts, I did not follow the lame conver-sation that was going on between my two companions. Hamda was ostensibly more drunk than Robert, and he was trying to explain to him in his rudimentary English how the Islamists got allied to the Mafia. In contrast, Robert nodded, unruffled and undisturbed by his ragged language. They were not sure they understood each other perfectly, but they seemed to get on well. For a moment, I pursued laconically their idle chat. I was lasciviously languishing while my eyes roamed purposelessly through the balcony over the neighbouring buildings. I was somewhat irritated, and I do not know why I kept looking now and then at my watch without really noticing the time. I stood up and went to look at the street from the balcony. The traffic seemed quite normal; the shops were open, and the passersby did not seem in a hurry. They were strolling indifferently along the shops-windows. Some would stop to look at the goods or chat with the merchants, whereas the others would continue their walk up to the next crossing, which forked two other branches of the street. In front of the hotel, on the opposite sidewalk, there is a stand of newspapers and magazines, where some people gather and linger to read the front pages or to leaf through the magazines. The stand-keeper and two of his assistants were eying them sullenly - I had already noticed their gaze when I was passing by - in case one took a copy under his armpit and slinked away. The street was dirty and dusty, as if it had not been scavenged for days. Even the few trees scattered hither and thither at the same distance from each other on the sidewalks seemed gaunt and asymmetric. There was something awkward and meticulous about their being there, displaying their frolic shades, but somewhat amorphous, ill-entertained, and sad. I knew there was a public square nearby; I had already spotted the sorrowful state of its lawn and vegetation. The wild weeds were climbing onto the trees and strangling their flowers and branches, and the wooden benches were decaying behind the rusty iron bars forming the enclosure. If the architect who erected such a square in that part of the town intended to make it more cheerful and less sad because of all the tedious walls hindering clear sight, I think he had failed. The pitiful state of the square demoralised me more than the passive platitude of the neighbouring buildings. Even the green of its overlaying foliage seemed outlandish, artificial, and altered to me. I do not know how those citizens I saw loafing on the lawn or idling on the benches could bear such an ostracising place. Ostensibly, they are not natives of the city. Perhaps, like me, they are somewhat exiled, cut off from their roots, because of the war, the military coups, or any other social plague or familial disaster. Perhaps they were homeless and found in that forlorn square the sole refuge hospitable, where they would wait for better days. The season of rains had not yet started; I wondered where all those displaced people would lodge with their wives and kids when the winter falls on the town. Then I recalled the manager of the hotel and grinned. He was certainly still waiting for my donation, and it dawned on me that I was not more reassured about my future than the hundreds, perhaps the thousands of have-not and homeless people raining on the city from their remote villages. For the first time, I contemplated that I am also an exile, and what is more scathing is that I am an exile in my own country. Yet, I am neither an expatriate nor an outcast. Until my detention, I have always lived in osmosis with my milieu. I was a respectable member of my society, a twig of the great tree that encompassed with its huge, shielding shade the whole country... An insider. Then something went wrong. My life, as well as that of my family, was being stormed by a sudden hurricane. In a short time, I lost everything: my post, social status, and family. The solid ground under my feet cracked and slumped like a soft jelly or a loose, flimsy lay of ice crinkling and melting down under the sun... All of a sudden, I was nobody.

*****

Five

I am aware that I am still nobody. The fact that I am living, at least transiently, in a five-star hotel may be misleading to whoever looks at me. But who is Bassam Bourasin in this strange, vast, wild, miscellaneous city? What is he doing here? What is his purpose? Where does he come from, and where is he heading? It seems odd that the only echo from my past, and thereby the unique assurance that I am not quite a straw in the wind, comes from the casual, unsolicited, and even dangerous presence of that drunk travesty, whom I never trusted or believed: Hamda La'war! And when he disappears, as he will undoubtedly do soon, all my past will sink in the burbling flood crossing the city, and the whole country, and with him will vanish the last relic from my native village and perhaps even my memory.

Suddenly and curiously, I discovered how grateful I was to my old enemy. I have no doubt that Hamda had never considered himself as my equal or my friend, for he had unscrupulously over-exploited my weakness and humble origins. He would very likely resume the same behaviour if, by any chance, we returned to our former situation, with me as a bank clerk in 'Ouja, and he as the mighty president of the party's cell. Nevertheless, I wondered who among the two men I had to trust when I compared him and Hassan. The former had enslaved me to his party and made of me the stooge of his ambition. The latter had merely instigated the murder of my mother and my fiancée and made of me also the instrument of his ambition. That both of them are detestable to me seemed the natural and logical consequence. Then I realised that to be myself, I had to be on my own and to get rid of them both as soon as it became possible; that would perhaps estrange me much more than I am, for I would lose two enemies at once, without however winning a new friend. But since I am already an exile, the loss would not be harmful. That is to say that one needs one's foes in the same measure that one needs one's friends, for without enmity and friendship, we never know who we indeed are. It is from the opposition of two wills that the light sparkles out and spreads over the way; then, if we can overcome our impotence and bypass the paradoxical situation, the issue would be outgoing.

My feeling of solitude did not decrease because of these lucubrations. I was more wistful, more gloomy and gaunt, more disheartened and flustered than I ever had been. Even in jail, I did not feel so abandoned by the mighty and benign providence, so orphan and afflicted by my fate, so induced to stick to the scant tribulation that overwhelmed me and enveloped my mind. I had something to cling to in jail. I was hoping because I knew I was innocent. I never believed that my indictment was serious, even when I shouted to Dalila in my despair that she might wait for twenty years before getting married. I still do not know why I behaved so sadistically, so cynically, so hypocritically with her when she was expecting that I lull her and ease her worries. I regret it bitterly now. Her warm tears will add a new burden to my already clogged loneliness. Poor Dalila! She had died believing that her beloved fiancé would rot in prison and that when he is released, it would be too late. Perhaps she had never abandoned the hope of seeing me again. The fact that she was still caring for my mother and was with her when the assassins broke in proves it. She would not have died if she remained with her parents. She would be at this very hour still living and very likely comforting me for the loss of my mother. I would not have felt so immeasurably condemned to loneliness and misery. But I will console myself again with that anachronical and amphibious Mektub, albeit I know it is a pitiful and paltry consolation. It costs nothing to believe that God is behind our darkest fate and that he doomed us willingly and purposely to test our stamina. Why does He need such a childish game? Is He so bored with His creation? Has He nothing else to do than to strike His weak creatures with ruthless calamities and to watch them scrambling and scrimmaging and vomiting their guts? Mektub! Is God a sadist, then? Is He a perverse Creator tormenting His slaves for the sake of His selfish pleasure? What has this to do with His infinite goodness, illimitable bounty, and boundless generosity? Mektub! This is quite an acataleptic, senseless, obsolete, and even dangerous word. It is an alibi for criminals, a justification for genocides of unredeemable human cruelty.

I wanted to believe in it, though. I thought I had no other option since I was impotent while undergoing the injustice. I had to cling to something, whether metaphysical nonsense or merely nonsense, whose vacuity is masked by a metaphysical rant, a simulacrum of reason, a hectic backlash of what is purported to appear reasonable. Islamic Commonsense, if it were! Popular sapience! Mobbish pre-science! What a braggart, desiccated, rusty duplicity! And I even played the comedy for myself! I tried to convince my reluctant, doubtful mind that Mektub is not an illusion but the only truth encompassing our existence. I told myself that I only have to admit it since I realise the ubiquity of the Almighty God. Afterwards, I plunged into my daydreams, married Dalila in the invisible world, decided that I was as capable as Haj Mukhtar to deal with Jins, spirits, and other poltergeists, exchanged my faltering - but yet tangible reason - for neurotic beliefs, and was even ready to step on the track of John Law and found a bank in the fictive world whose imaginative walls I have erected to surround me instead of the dismaying walls of the prison. Otherwise, I had unwillingly built a jail inside my jail, either to protect myself or to entertain the illusion that I was living an everyday life. I was dealing with the Invisibles. Yet, I have omitted that madness is also invisible, though it is pretty palpable.

My fictive jail grew gradually to encompass and even re-place the prison of stones and iron wherein I had been detained. And though I am no longer a justice convicted, I am still a prisoner of my foolishness. I am the jailed and the jailer. My mind, stuffed with wide ambitions, obsessed with quixotic ideas and jarring thoughts, squeezed with irrational fears, and tormented with contrition, guilt, shame, subjected to the yoke of the past, overloaded with blurring illusions and swathing quandary, confused by conceit, self-deception, mean-ingless tribulations, nagged and goaded by false premises and scant conclusions, seethed by abuses and humiliations, miffed, interlocked, provoked, revoked, has become the passive, lascivious, rabid prison of my soul, the graveyard of an apocryphal, unscrambled, hypochondriac hieroglyph. Enslaved to its ubiquitous dictatorship, I have been rambling for months aimlessly, abscind the real, dodging and dawdling along the squirming paths, raving about my life like a dotard, contemplating its havoc with sordid titillation, and a morbid fascination.

No, I am not yet dead. Would it be more honourable if I were? What had I been spared for? To be the condescending accomplice of the assassins of my mother and my fiancée, the destroyers of my nest, the extirpators of my roots? No, I am not dead - I see perfectly that I am not, damn it! But it is just as if I am.

I am no longer able to look at Hassan straight in the eyes without thinking that he had given the orders to murder those whom I loved, that his hands are stained with their blood, that neither his good intentions nor his coaxing promises could change anything to the putrescent, miasmic truth. What will I say to him when he comes? Is there still any choice left to me?

I lifted my head and stared at the blue sky of September. The sun is tired and sallow; its rays are still stabbing the drowning city, and the shades are slinking heavily on the silent walls, musty roofs, proud minarets, lazy domes, and shabby windows. This is the same sky I used to see through the rusty bars of my cell, envying the birds crossing its bright space for being so free, upright, and happy. And now it seems to me that it is not the same sky. It is not barred in my sight, yet the bars are inside my head, well fastened into my brain, deeply wedged like nails in a coffin. The voice of the Muezzin came over again through the metallic sound of the loudspeaker, calling the faithful to their duty. Behind me, I overhear the cackling laughter of my two companions, hoaxed with whisky. Allah is Great, and His mercy is immeasurable! Another glass of that paradisaic drink tempts me.

I returned to the room and poured another drink, which I took over to the balcony. Robert and Hamda gazed at me listlessly as I strolled across the room. The bottle was nearly empty; I did not feel the time elapsing. On the street, the traffic grew more animated. I noticed for the first time a little crowd gathering along the sidewalks. These souls, mostly in the vigour of youth, either swaggered past the gleaming shopfronts with no intent of commerce or stood statuesque beneath the sheltering boughs. Initially, my thoughts leaned towards the ordinary; perhaps they awaited conveyance. But the streets bore no vehicles for their service. Instead, they huddled in small and large groups, their stillness almost eerie in intensity.

Despite the mellowing effects of the whisky, I found my-self trapped in a mood of sullen contemplation. Yet, outside, a vendor's vexation contrasted sharply with my inertia. With a booming voice, he directed his young aides, who darted about their kiosk with the urgency of creatures trapped. I pondered this flurry of activity, this frenetic dance juxtaposed against the languid pace of the traffic. Cars, once swift, now moved as if against some intangible force. At the crossroads, the traffic lights' governance had faltered; vehicles stacked, and their impatient horns sang a cacophonous symphony.

As I fixed my gaze upon the scene, I noticed a surge from adjacent streets, a tide of humanity all moving with a singular purpose. From the university's direction, a multitude emerged, swelling the numbers of those already present. These movements, coupled with Robert's whispered tales of a gathering and the swift approach of police vehicles, painted a clear tableau: these youths, interspersed with a few women, were perhaps the very students caught in the anticipatory crosshairs of authority. Either denied the camaraderie of the campus or evicted from it, their presence on the street grew palpably. Shopfronts, sensing an impending storm, shuttered their windows and doors. The press stand nearby scrambled to safeguard its wares. The three men were busy arraying their merchandise and stocking it hurriedly inside their store. Vehicles grew restless, their horns piercing the thickening air. Both flanks of the street soon succumbed to the ever-increasing swell of bodies. This faceless sea of humanity, pulsating and alive, began to hum—a resonance building, overpowering the mechanical sounds, much like the tumultuous crashing of waves upon a storm-lashed coast under a shrouded moon.

Driven by a rising trepidation, I beckoned Robert and Hamda to my side, "Behold, the streets are now awash with the sea of humanity."

With a languid air, they strolled over; hands braced against the balustrade, their heads held back, seemingly apprehensive of the gales of change that threatened to blow. Below, the throng multiplied, surging, undeterred by the dwindling traffic.

"What the hell!" Robert exclaimed, voice thick with a mix of liquor and a mounting dread. "A demonstration!"

"A rebellion!" Hamda declared, almost jubilant. "The dawn of a new era! Did I not foretell the demise of these despots?"

"Keep quiet!" I chided, sensing danger, "The police will be upon us soon, and perhaps even the military. Don't triumph so fast! You're selling the bear's skin before killing it."

"Bloody hell! Janet is still outside in this tempest! How the devil will she navigate through this fevered throng? Look at them! It's madness incarnate!"

"Where had she ventured?"

"Likely the souks," he muttered.

"If she remains within the souks," I posited, "she's safe."

His gaze, awash with concern, met mine. "Your meaning?"

"The souks, nestled deep within the ancient Medina are safe. I don't believe the demonstrators intend to march on the Medina. All of the ministries are in the modern city; any disturbance will not reach the souks."

As we conversed, the shrill trill of the telephone pierced the atmosphere. After a moment's hesitation, I hurriedly attended to its call.

"Bassam, is that you?" A familiar gravelly voice asked. "I've heard tell of unrest near your quarters. How dire is it?"

Hassan. For a fleeting moment, I felt disconnected, almost inclined to sever the call. But his insistence pulled me back.

"Indeed, Hassan. The streets brim with thousands, and their number only swells."

A brief silence ensued.

"Well, don't worry. We're coming."

I heard at that moment the monotone roar of a propeller or perhaps several, for the noise was quite deafening, and I was forced to shout:

"It seems that your helicopters are already here. What are you going to do?"

A sardonic chuckle.

"What would you do if you were in my place?"

"I'm not in your place."

"I know, but what would you do?"

Contemplating, I answered, "Engage them. With words. Ask them to retreat, to delegate a voice for their concerns."

Another pause.

"We've tried. Their desires are amorphous, rooted in chaos. They're but puppets."

The clamour outside melded with the roar of the choppers, becoming almost indecipherable. From my vantage, Robert and Hamda remained transfixed by the relentless horde.

"I intended to extend an invitation," Hassan continued, "A soirée with Sophia, tonight."

"Tonight?" I retorted, incredulous. "We're besieged. How do you intend to breach this barrier?"

"Helicopters," he replied coolly, "Your helicopters."

Despite the turmoil, his calm resonated. He seemed untouched by the chaos.

"Is it imperative?" I queried.

"Not in essence, but one shouldn't alter one's course for mere trifles."

"Trifles? Thousands amass, inciting upheaval!"

"Order will be restored, the guardians of peace will ensure it."

"But are you not their leader?"

"Ah, misinterpretation," he corrected, "I helm National Security — the realm of secrets and shadows. Distinct from mere law keeping." He paused, "Would you like to have supper with me and Sophia? She's throwing a party where you can meet some powerful people. It's a nice opportunity for you to be introduced. I was going to take you in my car, but I now realise you have a driver. So, if you can find a way out, he knows where the villa is. The party starts around 8 p.m."

"And if not?"

"Trust," he replied, "All will be righted." Before I could respond, the line went dead.

***

Amid this maelstrom, Sophia's dinner seemed a distant, unlikely mirage. I casually glanced at the opulent timepiece that now adorned my wrist—a spoil from my chauffeur. Its luxury sat in stark contrast to its former owner. Perhaps, in some moral bartering, I should suggest to Hassan that the man's wages be augmented. The theft was not in my nature; however, the beast within me often roared in commerce.

The roar outside now rose to an overpowering crescendo. Hamda, shadowed by Robert, stumbled into the room. Both were flushed from liquor and the rush of adrenaline, their eyes wide, betraying a mixture of inebriation and excitement. The very walls vibrated with the outcry from the streets.

"What bellows from the masses?" I inquired of Hamda.

"They want peace, democracy, and amnesty for their comrades."

"Seems a simple enough demand."

"Simple? It's merely the dawn. When the workers and the unemployed rally with them, that will be the true showdown."

"Curbing your enthusiasm might be wise. Orchestrating a revolution isn't a child's play. Your allies from the south are nowhere in sight. These students, unarmed, are but gossamer against the might of the police force. I suggest you capitalise on this upheaval to slip away. This place won't shield you for long. Should they apprehend you here, you'll be ensnared. This uproar is your chance. Blend in, then make your escape. Your continued presence here is a peril you might live to rue."

He paused, searching for words, "Where do I go? Before crossing paths with you, I had shelter—a comrade's home. A buddy of mine, a trade unionist who is also one of our men. Everything was well until he vanished unexpectedly, and I have reason to believe he was being pursued by the police or militia. I fled the house since it was no longer secure; I was wandering aimlessly around town when I saw your car. Fortunately, his wife was not home; otherwise, borrowing her clothes would have been more difficult. Without this mask, I would be recognised; they have spread my photography and are for my head. It's hopeless. Either we pull them down in 24 hours or we're done."

"Don't daydream. You can't expect to bring them down without weaponry and an organised army. Where are the guns you mentioned? Where are your troops? Where are your friends? Where are the Americans and their money? Those youngsters you see down there will be crushed in two hours. Your revolution is a ruse. You should consider your own safety."

We were shouting to be heard. The roar of the crowd was growing increasingly overwhelming.

Robert had been silent until now, but his growing distress was palpable. With sudden resolve, he headed for the door, declaring, "I can't stand by any longer; Janet might be in danger."

"Where do you think you're going?" I inquired.

He paused, hand resting on the door handle, "I need to find her. She might not even be in the souks anymore. She could be in trouble."

"You won't get far. The streets are swarming with people and the police have likely blocked all routes. Plus, you're hardly inconspicuous, reeking of alcohol. They'll snag you instantly."

"My wife is out there! I can't just stay here, wringing my hands. I'd never forgive myself."

With determination, he pushed the door open and stepped out. On impulse, I called after him, "Robert! Hold on! I'll come with you."

Hamda, grasping the gravity of the situation, looked alarmed. "Where are you both headed?"

After briefly explaining, he said, "I'm coming too."

Surprised by his unexpected offer, I cautioned, "It could be dangerous for you. Maybe you should find another way."

"No other way exists. I'll follow my nephew."

"But you've been drinking."

"Damn it!" he cursed.

Seeing his determination, I asked for his gun. "Why?" he shot back.

"Don't make matters worse. If they catch you with it, it might be the end for you. Let me take it. If things go south, I can handle the consequences better than you can."

"You don't even know how to use it."

"I hope I won't have to. It's merely for peace of mind— just in case. And more importantly, to ensure you don't have it on you."

After some hesitation, Hamda handed over the gun concealed beneath his cloak. It felt heavy in my hand, undoubtedly loaded. I donned a tweed jacket and placed the gun in its pocket. Hamda followed, struggling slightly in his long attire, his face concealed by the veil.

Looking back, I can't pinpoint what propelled me into the chaos. Why did I feel compelled to accompany Robert in search of his wife? And why did I let Hamda tag along? As if that wasn't risky enough, I'd added to the peril by pocketing a loaded weapon. Was it genuine concern or sheer folly? Those questions didn't cross my mind then. Somehow, I felt a duty to help Robert and Janet. They were strangers in my homeland, and now, as friends, I felt responsible for their safety.

Robert was so concerned for her that he didn't wait for us. We had to hurry to catch up to him. Our sudden departure likely perplexed the other hotel guests and staff who witnessed it. The hotel manager, Mr. Ali, was in the lobby. He walked up to meet me with a friendly smile, trying to engage me in conversation. But I swiftly cut him off, "Sorry, Mr. Ali, I'm in a hurry. We'll chat later."

His confusion was evident as we swiftly moved past him, leaving him frozen like a bewildered statue. Outside, we found Robert looking despondent, scanning the chaotic scene beyond the hotel's gates. He stated the obvious, "We can't get out."

Hamda, surprising both of us, confidently said, "Follow me. I know another way."

Confidently, Hamda led the way through the parking lot, with us trailing quietly behind. Clearly, he was more familiar with the area than us. Amidst the tumultuous noise surrounding us, the distant thunder went unnoticed, its rumbling akin to a multitude of drums playing in unison. We couldn't communicate over the din when we finally registered the sound.

I could feel the changing atmosphere, the daylight taking on a dim and listless hue. While still evident in the sky, the sun was overshadowed by a thick layer of grey, formless clouds marching northward. Intermittent gusts of hot air met my face. The persistent heat and the oppressive atmosphere, contrasting starkly with the coolness of the hotel's interior, soon had sweat trickling down my forehead. Using my handkerchief, I dabbed away the sweat while keeping pace with Robert, following Hamda's trail.

We wound around the building, past the square, the pool, and the tennis court. The area, usually bustling with guests, was now relatively empty. Many had chosen the safety of the indoors, replacing their outdoor activities with indoor games or simply passing the time watching TV or reading in the lobby and coffee-house, waiting for calmer moments. Those we did encounter seemed unfazed by our hurried movement.

Eventually, we reached a more minor, seemingly unguarded gate at the back of the hotel. Despite its appearance of solitude, the distant shouts of protesters still reached our ears, leaving me wondering if our exit would genuinely lead us away from danger. Hamda paused, indicating the gate, and simply stated, "This is it."

With caution, I reached out to the gate's handle, turning it. The iron gate responded with a creak before giving way. As we ventured out, we found ourselves in a densely populated backstreet, which seemed less congested than the primary thoroughfare. We manoeuvred without having to push or jostle, weaving our way through the masses, hoping to find a less crowded route by reaching the next street.

But our hopes were dashed soon after. Before we could get to the street's end, we were engulfed by a tidal wave of students, their panic and fervour pulling us along with their frantic retreat back towards the main street. A formidable police force, armed to the teeth with cudgels, rifles, and machine guns, advanced towards us. As tensions escalated, some protesters began pelting the officers with stones, inciting the fury of a commanding officer. The noise drowned his shout, but its implications were clear when, moments later, gunshots pierced the air, some aimed at the ground, seemingly to target our feet.

A distressing cry reached my ears. I glanced back, spotting Hamda faltering and eventually falling to the ground. He struggled, attempting to stand, but ultimately resigned to crawling. My instincts screamed for me to return and assist him. Yet, the echoing gunfire and the bullets ricocheting off walls held me back. I rushed forward, only to be carried away by the multitude like a straw in a raging sea. I was in the middle of the storm, dragged along by an invisible force. Everywhere I looked, hands reached out, gripping my arms, shoulders, and wrists, pulling me into the tumultuous sea of humanity. As I was thrust into the thick of it, I quickly realised the futility of resistance. We moved as one, a singular mass of emotion and energy, and it was impossible to distinguish one from another. The din around me was deafening – a mix of shouts, cries, and unintelligible chatter. The street walls felt oppressive, like prison barriers closing in. I wished they'd crumble under the weight of our collective desperation. It felt like we were both the audience and the actors in a macabre play, the lines between reality and performance blurring. As the crowd's enthusiasm grew, it became evident that there was no control or direction. We were consumed by a frenzy, driven by a force that desired only chaos and destruction.

The realisation hit me like a ton of bricks: there was no escape from this nightmare. We had become one with the mob, lost in its madness. The clarity of this thought barely registered amidst the tumult. Waves of emotions washed over me – fear, anger, hatred, and more. My heart raced with an unprecedented mix of rage, anger and helplessness. The sheer magnitude of our collective lack of control was overpowering. It was as if we were mere puppets, our strings pulled by a sinister force lurking within us.

The reality dawned on me in the heart of the mayhem. We were adrift in a sea of chaos, our wills swallowed up by the over-whelming power of the masses. And somewhere in this roiling mass was the puppeteer, the unseen force driving us, though its identity remained elusive.

***

Six

I couldn't see the Sheraton's towering, strong, reassuring walls, the lush green of the trees, or the soothing blue of the sky.. As fruitless and pointless as they are, the few landmarks I had gathered throughout my brief stay in the city allowed me to trace evidence of my existence and postulate that I am, in fact, the man I think I am, damaged and fading away. I was sprinting through the bituminous, damp, congested streets of an unknown city with flocks of people, bustling wrathfully and grappling with the upsetting aught that I didn't notice I was soaked from head to toe. A fine drizzle was splattering the pavement, the walls, the shop windows and the trees, and murky grey water trickled down the pavements in flakes and thin streams. Although the dense crowd had dissipated, I could still hear the snickering of bullets, mob cries, and the ululations of police sirens and ambulances. We were racing in clusters, and the rain was pelting our faces. I shifted my gaze backwards. Long red tongues of fire clambered, danced, and stretched obscenely in humpy dumpy clouds of black smoke hauling and hitching about the roadway. I carried on running.

The grim aftermath of the city's turmoil unfolded before

my eyes. Storefronts lay shattered, engulfed in flames as parked cars became unwitting torches, and the tumultuous crowd swept through the streets, wreaking havoc and leaving destruction in its wake. I found myself darting from one street to the next, desperately seeking refuge from the chaotic mob and the heavy-handed police presence, but sanctuary proved elusive. Doors were firmly shut, and building entrances were sealed off. Law enforcement officers obstructed every escape route, resorting to live ammunition against protesters, no longer aiming at their feet. The result was a grim procession of casualties, with wounded individuals crawling amidst the chaos and the survivors inadvertently treading upon lifeless bodies strewn across the desolate asphalt. Once innocently splashed by our hurried steps, the rain-soaked pavement now bore a haunting crimson hue. Barricades, fashioned from the wheels of any available cars and buses, obstructed the paths of rioters and police alike. These makeshift barriers were set ablaze when the authorities advanced, hindering their progress. Unfortunately, the fires soon spiralled out of control, engulfing nearby structures. Terrified residents were forced to abandon their homes, navigating the streets with trepidation. In their desperation, they found themselves entangled with the police, who, with little hesitation, opened fire, often mistaking these innocent civilians for rioters in the chaos.

The scene before me resembled a chilling tableau from a horror film. It was as if humanity had regressed to a primal state, with women and children falling victim to unforgivable violence akin to rabid beasts. It was too late for the police to prevent this nightmarish tragedy. As I approached the harrowing scene while still in a sprint, I couldn't help but contrast it with the hypocritical and discordant metropolis it had once been. Instead, I witnessed again the beloved yet battered 'Ouja, marred by rampant arson and unparalleled unrest.

Just a few paces away, a young mother lay sprawled on the street, cradling her newborn child tightly to her chest. Strikingly, she was not veiled. I came to an abrupt halt and knelt beside her, observing that she was still breathing, though her words remained inaudible. She appeared to be in her early twenties, not much different in age from Dalila. I attempted to pry the infant from her grasp gently, but she clung to the child with a fierce determination as if he were a lifeline in the tumultuous sea of violence that surrounded us.

"Are you alright?" I inquired with genuine concern, though the absurdity of my words was not lost on me. Nevertheless, she offered no response. Desperate to assist her to her feet, I made a futile attempt. It was then, as I grasped her shoulders to prevent her from collapsing, that she raised her head and regrettably expelled a horrifying spurt of blood. I gazed upon the baby's pallid and bloated visage. His eyes, devoid of life, stared vacantly, and his tiny mouth was agape, frozen in a silent sob, as if on the verge of crying. It was the same bullet that had pierced his mother's chest that had now lodged in the baby's heart, silencing his potential cries forever. With the mother's head tilting back, there remained nothing more to bear witness to in that tragic moment.

Slowly, I rose from my crouched position, a morbid fascination lingering as I withdrew from the sombre tableau I had just observed. After covering a few meters, I turned back to face the two lifeless bodies, locked in a final, unyielding embrace, even in death. Raindrops pelted their now skeletal forms as people scattered in all directions to escape the terrifying storm of bullets raining down upon them. The police closed in, their gunfire echoing in my ears so closely that I momentarily believed I had been hit. Reacting instinctively, I fled the scene, raising my hand to shield my ear as if seeking solace in that futile gesture of self-protection.

I lost all sense of time and place; my direction was unknown, and I followed the fleeing crowd blindly. The street stretched endlessly, or perhaps it did end, only to lead us to another or even back to where we began. Were we trapped in a never-ending loop? I now recall seeing the lifeless bodies of that woman and her baby multiple times as I sprinted through the chaos. It was inconceivable that they could have been shot down on every street corner; it defied reason. Perhaps I was hallucinating, perhaps it was a different woman each time... But such a notion was implausible! I couldn't convince myself otherwise. I'm sure that as long as I ran, that haunting image persisted. Periodically, I encountered a lifeless woman lying on the rain-soaked pavement, clutching her child with an unyielding grip, their pallid faces bathed in a grim mixture of rain and blood. Gradually, my flight ceased to be from the police bullets; instead, it became a desperate escape from the relentless sight of that woman cradling her baby, reminiscent of Mary holding the infant Jesus. I can't explain why their presence filled me with such dread that I averted my gaze when I sensed their presence on the opposite side of the street, as if they lay there in their tragic tableau of rain and blood, waiting for me to approach and futilely attempt to raise the mother to her feet. In vain! She would gaze at me, her expression one of helplessness, and instead of vomiting blood, she would break into hysterical laughter. Her head would then fall back, and I would hastily rise to my feet and scurry away, only to stop and glance back at her. I would resume running, bullets whizzing past and the endless street stretching before me. The city opened its gates like a gaping furnace, ready to consume me. The rain relentlessly pounded my face, and I felt ensnared in this desperate escape.

Suddenly, a hand clamped onto my arm, halting my aimless sprint, and a familiar voice called out:

"Bassam! Where have you been, for Heaven's sake? Are you alright?"

It was Robert, drenched and dishevelled, his clothes torn, and his face smudged as if it had been greased. Recognising him was a challenge, but his eyes and fair hair ultimately confirmed his identity, though his voice alone would have sufficed.

I exclaimed, "Thank God, you're alive, Robert!"

He chuckled, "Yes, I've got a thick skin, too thick for bullets!"

My concern shifted to Janet. A shadow passed over his eyes, and he scanned the surroundings cautiously. I hadn't noticed that I had unwittingly entered a narrow alley, but following his gaze, I realised we were in a dead-end. Fortunately, it was empty. Distant gunshots and cries persisted, indicating that the chaos had not yet subsided. He grabbed my arm and urged me to follow him.

"Come on, we can't stay here. It's too dangerous."

We entered an arched doorway, finding ourselves within the dim corridor of what appeared to be an old building. While I struggled to adjust to the darkness, Robert fumbled along the wall momentarily. It was then that I noticed evening casting its shroud over the city. Outside, darkness had also fallen, but the electric streetlights battled against the rain and the night. Eventually, Robert found the switch, and a faint, yellowish bulb dangled from the ceiling, illuminating the corridor. I spotted a staircase and settled down on the steps. Robert joined me, leaning his back against the railing in silence for a moment before he asked:

"Do you have any cigarettes?"

I delved into my pockets. "Yes, I must have some." I retrieved a cigarette pack from my inner jacket pocket and ensured it remained dry. I handed him one and took another for myself. We lit our cigarettes, enveloped in the chilly air of the narrow, dingy-walled corridor. Occasionally, distant gunshots shattered the sombre evening silence, but the sounds of the mob had faded by then. I inquired:

"How did you find this refuge?"

"It wasn't easy," he replied. "I hid under a car parked on a nearby street when the helicopters began firing at the crowd..."

I interrupted him, my tone sullen, "I didn't realise the helicopters were involved."

"They were, indeed," he continued. "Bullets were raining down from the sky!"

I was on the verge of apologising, for officially, I was the one who had brought those helicopters to the country. However, when I had signed the contract, I had no clue the police would use them to cause such mass casualties. Besides, the contract was a sham. I couldn't be held accountable for the misuse of those helicopters, and expressing an apology would have seemed odd, shocking and misplaced.

"The car I was hiding under caught fire," Robert said, "so I had to flee and wandered until I found my way here. But something struck me. When I was under that car, I observed everything happening in the street, and now I'm convinced it wasn't the students who turned the demonstration into a violent riot; it was the police."

I inquired, "Why are you so certain?"

"Because the students weren't armed, were they? However, the police began shooting at them. Then I saw a group of men approaching from another street, and it appeared they were all Islamists, identifiable by their beards and their handling of clubs, sticks, and possibly even guns."

"Do you mean the Islamic Militia?"

"Very likely. Those men I saw were the ones who initiated the fires; they set wheels and entire cars ablaze in the streets, shattered shop windows with iron bars and motorcycle chains. They rampaged for a significant period without police interference. Then, they withdrew, leaving the place in flames and covered in blood; it was only at that point that the police intervened."

"It's strange, but not entirely surprising," I responded. "They are capable of such duplicity; in any case, it serves their interests."

"Why would it serve their interests?"

I recalled my conversation in 'Ouja with the Indian.

"Well, it's a complex story. In reality, the Islamists are not as united as they may appear. They are divided into factions, each vying for more power and privileges. For instance, the Chief of the Militia may be at odds with the Director of Security, which suggests that he may have unleashed his men to create trouble for his rival. I wouldn't be surprised if I learned that the Afghan - I mean, the leader of the Militia - had orchestrated this chaos.

He likely has his supporters, even within the university... although there are other possibilities."

Robert pondered this for a moment. "Not unlikely," he conceded. "Many students are undoubtedly Islamists, and it's odd that they would participate in a riot against the government unless not all of them are involved. The situation is quite murky. I was astonished to see them, you know, and I hadn't considered the possibility of an internal government struggle."

"If you witnessed the Islamic Militia, there's no doubt about their involvement. It's unmistakable."

"Jesus! I not only saw them, but I'd bet my right hand that they are the culprits who set the city ablaze. I'm certain they would have killed me if they had caught me. I've seen everything they'd want to hide."

"They most likely would have. But what about Janet now?"

"Yes, let's go and check the souks."

Robert extinguished his cigarette beneath his shoe and stood up. I followed him onto the street. The night seemed quieter, but the drizzle persisted, pelting the pavement.

As we emerged from the alley, he asked, "Where's your aunt?"

I hadn't anticipated the question, as I had forgotten entirely about Hamda.

"Oh, don't worry about her," I replied. "By now, she's probably at the police station. They'll assist her in getting home. I'm better off without her."

Robert chuckled, seemingly unaware that a bullet near the hotel had hit Hamda.

"It appears she's quite familiar with the Sheraton!"

"Yes, indeed. It's her go-to spot whenever she's in the city."

He hesitated. "Is she... um... always fond of the... um..."

"Well, not consistently. But who knows? I don't see much of her, you know."

His expression remained unchanged, but I thought he was harbouring suspicions.

"You probably shouldn't have allowed her to follow us, although I'm not sure how we would have escaped without her help. If she's indeed at the police station, I doubt they'll be very kind to her... you understand, she was inebriated!"

"Oh, yes! But if she receives a few slaps on her big buttocks, it won't hurt her. It might teach her a valuable lesson, so that in the future, she refrains from imitating men's behaviour!"

He chuckled and replied, "Ah, well!"

***

30th September ...

Tomorrow, I'm going back to work at the bank... or rather, I'm going to finish my career in the Capital I used to despise. Everything is fine, and there is no reason for it to be otherwise. If I were a writer, I would have begun my novel with the hero's incarceration and ended it with his return to his bank, or more precisely, his promotion to a new position in the Capital. That is the happy ending, but even though I am getting there, I am not there yet. Fortunately! It is true that I am not a real hero but rather a fictive one. But it doesn't matter, since, anyway, I will be decorated. Eh! A national hero without war or fighting! That's as appealing as a genuine vocation would be. Hamda received his honorific medal after cuckolding his shoemaker neighbour. A great deed that went on the record as a notable sacrifice for the nation. I'll acquire the same medal for a phoney price in helicopters I never saw, let alone bought. The nation will be thankful to me, just as it was to Hamda for doing much less than I did. The time has come for such immense rewards.

I had not only performed my civil duty for many years without expecting anything in return from the State - which, I recognise, is absurd because these services are compensated - but I had also been the scapegoat of internal power struggles between men I hardly knew, and if I did, I hardly trusted, although I professed to be loyal to them. I am not just refer-ring to Hamda and his party but also to those who still hold power - I am referring to the Islamists, who had not been not ousted as Hamda wished. The riot was in vain. A great deal of damage and casualties, horrifying bloodshed, a foreboding and terrifying metamorphosis of the city into a sobbing, howling bottomless pit of human remains, an open racked place for the demon's kinks... May Allah's kindness be upon us! What a shambles! What nonsense! And that horrible, gory erroneous-ness was muffled under the hypocritical veil of reciprocal griev-ances, recriminations, apologies, promises, and hand-shaking between government members and students' representatives. We all smiled and relaxed as we watched them meet on our TV screens. Nothing felt more distant to them than the fact that hundreds of people had died, and they were not all rioters. They pretended not to be interested in death figures. What were all those people killed for? It wasn't the question to ask. Who cared or dared to? Everyone had realised that there was no sense in digging a ground completely swollen with excrements while we were all treading on it and attempting to hide its miasmic effluvium with a flowery carpet, and thus, great reconciliation was taking place.

I'm not complaining. God, no! Peace is always better, even if it means forgetting the dead and forgiving their killers! Forgetting the killed is less dangerous than forgetting their killers. We should be grateful, for we survived. We watched in awe as the kids were welcomed at the Presidential Palace like National Heroes. I must add that they had not been adorned as we had hoped, but I am confident this will not be a problem.

Abdelghani Abdelghaffar, wearing his customary black spectacles, sported a military uniform adorned with many medals befitting a General. It left me pondering the origins of those decorations festooning his chest. As far as I could recall, they couldn't have been earned on a battlefield. Our country had not seen any major conflict. And if one were to reminisce about the 1967 war against Israel, I struggled to identify any reason our officers should be rewarded for their conspicuous absence from the actual battlefield—unless, perhaps, the defeated were also being decorated!

But Abdelghani is a man of integrity. I doubted he would embellish himself with accolades for fictitious deeds unless our military heroes were just as fictitious as their civilian counterparts! True, he squints quite dramatically, but that alone should not justify self-promotion. After some contemplation, I arrived at two potential scenarios. Perhaps, like Hamda La'war, he had been involved in a dubious affair involving another man's spouse, which left him cross-eyed after a confrontation with the aggrieved husband—but still, he managed to secure his decorations. Alternatively, his comrades might have rewarded him with numerous medals following a successful coup against the Scoundrel. Regardless, there was no denying his merit. He was undoubtedly the right man in the right place.

As the saying goes, sometimes the most common of clichés holds wisdom. Is he not still combating the Scoundrel who threatens to transform our peaceful nation into a graveyard? That Genghis Khan of ours had not yet conceded defeat. He hopes to return to power, although I wish he never would. I was confident that our brave soldiers would make short work of him. I had good reason to believe so, as my brother-in-law informed me that we had recently received new supplies of weapons and aircraft. We were bolstered. Moreover, the fuel shortage, which had significantly hindered our war effort, was no longer an obstacle, thanks to our friendly neighbours who generously agreed to supply us with whatever we needed. Naturally, this assistance was not without conditions. We would need to reciprocate when the civil war concluded and our enemies were defeated.

For one thing was certain: our neighbours held no affection for the Scoundrel, and his vision of a secular regime with all its Western trappings rankled them. They recognised him as a liar, but what if his rhetoric deceived their populations? It would not be the first time a charlatan had led millions astray with falsehoods and empty slogans, just as Hitler had done, albeit through a relatively democratic election process. However, our Scoundrel's ascent began with the king's deposition and the republic's proclamation. Subsequently, he dismantled the constitution, promising to replace it with a modern one inspired by European models. Meanwhile, we were left in a constitutional vacuum, with the President as the sole source of law.

Ultimately, he would have set the entire region ablaze with subversion if he had remained in power. Such chaos at their borders was intolerable to our conservative neighbours. Thankfully, some determined patriots, moved by the suffering gradually imposed upon our people, took action. General Abdelghani Abdelghaffar led the charge who, despite his optical handicap, commandeered his illustrious tank and launched an audacious assault on the presidential palace one fateful night.

Unfortunately, the Scoundrel managed to elude capture, while Abdelghani, blinded by the labyrinthine corridors of the vast palace, pursued one of the bodyguards, mistaking him for the fugitive. In the heat of the moment, he shot the bodyguard down, believing he had killed the former president. The jubilant news was hastily relayed to television and radio journalists, who eagerly broadcasted it. It was a regrettable error but one for which Abdelghani could hardly be held accountable. He had a compelling excuse: his pronounced squint, a fact known to all his colleagues. They should have approached the delicate matter of assaulting the palace with more sense, which might have prevented the Scoundrel's escape. Alas, it was too late now. Yet, all our current predicaments undeniably trace their origins back to one source: the darkness of that night and the squinting eyes of General Abdelghani!

I was drawn to the President, not realising how highly regarded he was by our neighbouring nations. It's clear that nobody truly grasped his significance before the Coup. To compensate for our earlier ignorance, we now shower him with more exuberant displays of loyalty. The General's portraits, adorning shops, walls, and public spaces multiply in number and size each day. We're gradually uncovering the man's true stature and expressing our gratitude for his efforts to rescue us from the vile Scoundrel and bring peace to our nation. Even a whimsical rumour is circulating that the General doesn't squint; instead, he bears the "Hawar Al-zine," the unmistakable mark of beauty! Nonetheless, all depictions of the President continue to feature his trademark black glasses. While I haven't seen a painted portrait, I'm confident that the country's finest artists are working, capturing various aspects of the President's features.

My focus has shifted towards all the varied presidential life's splendid and noble facets since my marriage. Naturally, I now find myself happily settled in the very heart of my beloved wife, just as I am securely anchored in the heart of my beloved country—the Capital—while maintaining a solid connection to my cherished bank. I've become an actual Capitalist in every sense of the term. I own a significant sum of money and some properties, making me a capitalist in the financial sense. Moreover, I reside in the Capital, which solidifies my status. The days when I felt like a refugee, akin to the thousands of homeless individuals, are behind me. My marriage to Sophia has ended my feelings of being an outcast or in exile. It has thrust me into the forefront of society. By marrying the former Minister's divorcee, I've essentially taken his place—not yet in the Ministry, admittedly, but Sophia is convinced I possess the qualities of a great statesman. She's determined to use her influence as a Minister-maker to secure my best position. In the meantime, my new and genuine career has just commenced. I must be a devoted and supportive husband to rise swiftly and ascend to great heights.

I'm in no rush. Currently, I hold the position of Chief of

the Transfer and Exchange Department at the bank. However, it's merely a nominal role. I'm not obligated to show up at the office daily, nor am I required to do substantial work when I do. This is, in essence, an aristocratic post-tailor-made for me. I receive a full Chief of Department's salary, and my role primarily involves overseeing my team's work. "Just take a look and sign whatever papers they show you," Mr Khalil advised me. "Don't trouble yourself with reading everything; we have people specially trained for that task. Your job is simply to sign, Mr. Bassam."

Furthermore, I now hold a position on the bank's board. I attend board meetings alongside other directors. I am not yet a high-ranking boss, but a boss nonetheless. However, I've reached a point where I don't even need to actively work, as my wife is wealthy, although I'm uncertain about the extent of her wealth. I haven't delved into her bank accounts to compare her assets and mine; it's a sensitive matter. Nevertheless, I'm aware that if I require funds for my projects, she will offer her support. We are, in a sense, partners. My $200,000 is now at my complete disposal in the bank. On this front, Hassan has kept his promise admirably. Sophia knew I intended to embark on a construction enterprise and that repairs at the 'Ouja bank would commence soon. She's eager to assist me in realising this cherished project.

In reality, my primary occupation today is excelling in my role as a husband. I had no idea such a profession existed before marrying Sophia. She doesn't compensate me monetarily, but there are various rewards for fulfilling my duties well. I wouldn't have delayed my marriage if I had known about it earlier. Engaging in such intriguing careers should ideally commence early in life. (Of course, my perspective was quite the opposite during my time in prison, but I was inexperienced then.) It's never too early to excel, and it's certainly more appealing than toiling as a bank clerk for a meagre salary. I don't renounce my previous job; I don't deny that I found contentment as a clerk at the 'Ouja bank. However, at that time, I was oblivious to the realities of life. Sophia convinced me that if I aimed to ascend in society, I needed to relinquish the inconsequential role of a village bank clerk, which didn't align with my newfound status as the former Minister's spouse. When I asked her, "What should I do then?"

"You're so honest, my dear," she giggled. "Does that pose a problem?"

"Yes," I replied. "I don't know any other job."

"I'll give you one," she said, "be my husband."

"Is that a job for a man, Sophia?"

"Do you mean that it is more convenient for a woman?"

"That's not what I mean, dear," I said, laughing at the joke. But, when asked about his business, a guy cannot simply answer, "I am the husband of my wife."

"Why not? That is the job that every man in the country will envy you for, my dear. Isn't that what they do for the Queen's husband?"

That was it!

I am embarking on a new career with high hopes of swift advancement. My boss—by which I mean my wife—is exceptionally encouraging. She already envisions me as a Minister in President Abdelghaffar's government. This burgeoning interest and involvement in the exhilarating political arena continue to draw me closer to the top, which I believe is the right path.

Sophia is enthusiastic about propelling me rapidly towards success and the pinnacle of power. She expressed sympathy for my perceived misfortune when I casually mentioned the helicopter deal. In her view, I should have demanded at least fifty per cent of the agreement. She made it clear that the one hundred million dollars that went into her ex-husband's pocket as his share of the deal were ill-gotten gains, a sentiment I agreed with. But what about the other hundred million pocketed by her brother? She remained silent on that matter. However, she did blame Hassan for allowing Mamduh to claim half of the bid, although she didn't confront him directly. I explained to her that Hassan couldn't have acted independently and profited from clandestine deals behind the Minister's back without the tacit agreement and protection of his boss—Mamduh. I emphasised that selfishness is detrimental to both politics and business. Sophia responded with a shrug and a moment of contemplation. I continued, stressing the importance of placing national interests above personal considerations. She yawned and quipped, "Well, next time you're involved in a major business deal, please remember that seeking my advice is in the national interest. Okay?"

I'm sure she's right. A statesman-maker like her is never short of good ideas. As the ex-wife of a sitting Minister and the potential wife of the next one, she's ideally positioned to discern the national interest better than anyone else. I mustn't overlook the fact that she's also the sister of the National Security Director, which further bolsters her credentials. I've discovered a true treasure in her—goodwill, wisdom, patience, and tenderness.

Sophia is a bit older than me and already has three children

—two daughters and a son. However, the few years of difference between us aren't daunting or unsettling. I've found that marrying an older woman has its advantages. She generously shares her extensive life experience, allowing her husband to be both her adoptive son and husband simultaneously. Having lost both my mother and fiancée in the tragedy of 'Ouja, I've found a woman kind enough to fill both roles in my heart and mind in Sophia. Consequently, my life has taken a decisive turn.

We married quickly, just a week after our introduction, as if we had wasted enough time before our meeting and could no longer bear to be apart. Later, Sophia confessed it was love at first sight. I told her I was flattered and honoured, which was true. I added that I had an affection for her even before we met, which was a fabrication. She was delighted and intrigued, wondering how is it possible to love someone without seeing. I playfully replied, "That's the secret of men; women love at first sight, whereas we can fall in love from afar."

The wedding ceremony was far more straightforward than I had anticipated during all those years I was betrothed to Dalila. On the appointed day, I accompanied Hassan and some friends to the city's grand mosque. We sat on the mat before the sheikh, who recited some verses from the Koran. After the prayer, we formed a circle, and the sheikh declared me married to Sophia, instructing me to sign the marriage contract, which I did. The ceremony was brief and straightforward. Once the religious rites were complete, we left the mosque, climbed into our cars, and drove to the house where Sophia and other women awaited us. The same ritual occurred there, with the bride signing the contract. Guests enjoyed refreshments, sampled cakes, engaged in conversation, shared laughter, offered their congratulations, and gradually departed the house, one by one.

Sophia's children were present at the wedding, although they seemed oddly subdued. Being grown-up individuals, they didn't cause any disruptions. I had initially expected some resistance, but I quickly realised I was mistaken. Murad, the eldest at twenty years old, appeared largely indifferent. He congratulated me politely, kissed his mother, and went to his room casually as if I were a passing guest who happened to be temporarily in the house and would soon depart. I didn't interact with him much after that. When I asked Sophia, she explained that he typically spent most of his time outside and only returned in the evening. He often dined alone in his room while watching TV or listening to music. Occasionally, we shared breakfast in the kitchen, but he seldom engaged in conversation. He ate quickly, skimmed through magazines and newspapers (we receive many every day), uttered a word or two like "Please, pass the marmalade," and then strolled into the corridor. Initially, I thought he didn't like me, but Sophia reassured me that he grew up shy and reserved since he was a teenager. Moreover, he was absorbed in planning for his future career. He was preparing to leave the country for England or the USA. He had applied to some universities and was awaiting their responses before choosing. I learned yesterday that an American university had accepted him, although I don't know which one. Nevertheless, I wish him the best of luck.

The two girls were equally reserved, polite and empathetic. Thuraya, the elder at seventeen, resembled her father in appearance, although she didn't share his incessant verbosity. Zohra, who was fourteen, struck me with her likeness to Hassan. She had red hair, clear eyes, a slender frame, freckles, and lively, cheerful manners, much like a refreshing spring breeze. I felt a deeper affection for her than for the other two, and I believe she reciprocated my feelings.

This is my new family, and I've already grown accustomed to them. Another advantage of my marriage to Sophia is that I wouldn't need to press for children; they were already waiting for me. I had to say 'yes' to becoming a father and husband, and I eagerly embraced that role.

Sophia is a remarkable partner for any man with ambition and determination. Not only is she the ex-wife of a Minister (and potentially the wife of the next one), but she has also borne three children—a tangible testament to her fertility, which is highly prized. She is financially independent and well-regarded in the elite circles of the Capital. Moreover, she is beautiful and looks far younger than her actual age. She is small and slender yet exudes dynamism and vivacity. Her delicate features frame her brown hair, which cascades gracefully over her shoulders, giving her the aura of a humming Siamese cat. Her black eyes hint at the exotic, reminiscent of Far Eastern Asians. At the same time, her nose is elegantly sculpted and gracefully elevated above a small mouth, a straight chin, and two high, rosy cheekbones. It struck me immediately that she bore little resemblance to her ruddy, green-eyed brother. Nonetheless, her strong chin, firm lips, and unwavering gaze suggest her determination and relentless nature—a determination that led her to marry me, a future minister in the waiting, despite the likelihood that I was not the first man to propose to her after her divorce. And I said 'yes' because, after Hamda La'war's public confession, there was no point in stubbornly denying the truth. Since Hassan had proven his innocence and clean hands in the 'Ouja massacre, I resolved to move forward and propose to his sister, strengthening our nascent alliance with familial ties, as blood was on the verge of shattering it.

***

Seven

Two days after the unsettling riot had shaken the very core of our city, I found myself in a state of profound shock and fascination as I beheld Hamda La'war baring his soul on the television screen. My amazement was only heightened by the whisky that Robert and I had been partaking in. It was Robert's third and final bottle, and we had gathered to celebrate Janet's safe "return" and bid her and Robert farewell as their departure from the country was imminent.

In truth, our quest to locate Janet in the bustling markets and winding streets of the city that fateful night proved to be an exercise in futility. She had, in fact, never ventured beyond the sanctuary of our hotel. Initially, she informed Robert of her intention to step out to do some shopping. Still, a change of heart led her to explore the hotel's collection of shops, where she whiled away a considerable portion of the afternoon. Later, she ascended to the hotel's exhibition room, where discussions on the finer nuances of art engaged her with fellow patrons. Among them was a British-educated lady who, in a spontaneous gesture, extended an invitation for a rendezvous at the hotel's coffee shop. Consequently, while we were out navigating the rain-soaked streets amidst the cacophony of bullets, fearing the worst for her safety, Mrs Waterbird was comfortably ensconced in the coffee shop in the company of a mysterious Arab lady. Despite her traditional attire, the Arab lady, as it turned out, was an educator, well-versed in English literature and culture, who had previously resided in the heart of London. A swift camaraderie blossomed between Janet and her newfound friend based on their shared experiences and interests. The Arab lady expressed a keen desire to meet Robert, admired his painting, and wished to acquire one of his creations. However, Robert seemed to have vanished into thin air, possibly quenching his thirst in my room's solitude or traversing the abyss alongside me. Eventually, the Arab lady handed Janet a cheque along with her contact details, and Janet pledged to reach out for a dinner appointment.

Naturally, Robert and I found the bustling markets eerily bereft of life, akin to the vacant thoughts of a soul adrift in the void. Customers had deserted the labyrinthine alleys, and shopkeepers had secured their establishments for the night. Yet, amid this desolation, a solitary café still beckoned with its dimly lit ambience. We sat on the terrace and ordered two cups of robust Turkish coffee. The establishment exuded an air of melancholy, with only a handful of patrons leisurely puffing on their nargile pipes, their gaze adrift in the dimly illuminated street, a mere echo of its daytime vibrancy. Behind the counter, an elderly gentleman, etched with the creases of time, appeared engrossed in his ledger and a diminutive calculating device. He would lift his head at intervals, cast a weary glance at the street, and absentmindedly stroke his drooping moustache with a bony forefinger. Adorning the central wall, a prominent poster featured President Abdelghani grinning broadly and baring a complete set of teeth. The narrow street, paved with polished cobblestones, obscured any view of the night sky as a vaulted ceiling enveloped the entire thoroughfare, shrouding the celestial realm from sight. However, the haunting call of the muezzin, summoning the faithful to the fifth prayer of the day, resonated from a nearby minaret, its haunting melody slicing through the stillness of the night.

The waiter delivered our two cups of coffee and two glasses of water, as I had requested. Robert asked me to inquire about Janet's whereabouts, hoping the waiter or somebody had seen her. There was a slim chance, perhaps one in a thousand, that the observant waiter might have caught a glimpse of her presence in the markets that afternoon, and we could ill afford to let such a possibility slip through our fingers. I asked the waiter. He shook his head solemnly and replied, "No, sir, I did not see a solitary foreign lady. They usually cross these lanes in small groups, you know."

I endeavoured to describe Janet to him as vividly as possible, enlisting Robert's assistance to convey the nuances of her attire. He pondered momentarily, running his fingers through his hair, then ultimately shook his head in defeat. Our efforts had proved futile. With a sense of resignation, we released him from our quest, and he promptly gathered the scattered tables and chairs strewn across the terrace, stacking them in the corner of the café. We hastily consumed the remnants of our drinks, settled the bill, and left.

We traversed the winding market alleys, our spirits weighed down by exhaustion and the burden of a long and trying day, arriving on the other side of the city—the modern neighbourhood. We strolled silently, our gaze fixed upon the ambulances, their sirens still wailing as they transported the wounded, and the police vehicles weaving through the streets like a stitching needle in a tattered fabric. It was a sad duty, bearing witness to the aftermath of the catastrophe. Numerous people had been injured, many others had met a tragic end, and hundreds of students found themselves confined behind bars.

At a nondescript street corner, a vigilant police patrol intercepted us. The officer, displaying an air of authority, requested our identification papers. Robert promptly produced his passport while I fumbled through my pockets in a frantic search for my wallet. Alas, my haste had led to a crucial oversight; I had carelessly left it behind in my room. Instead, my fingers brushed against a cold, unyielding object in my pocket. Startled, I withdrew my hand with a swiftness that mirrored the sting of a scorpion's bite, my emotions inadvertently etched across my countenance. The officer considered me with a wary eye and snapped:

"We are awaiting your papers." He extended his hand and inquired, "Are you feeling well?"

"Oh, yes... thank you, sir," I stammered in response, my voice trembling as I continued, "I... the papers... Sorry! I believe I've forgotten my wallet..."

I was likely shaking. That was not only due to the chill of the evening air that had penetrated my bones or the dampness of my clothing that caused me to sneeze intermittently but also because, on that very day of turmoil, I happened to have a revolver, with neither identification papers nor a firearm license. My predicament was dire. I could already envision myself being escorted back to the confines of a prison cell. Dahdah,

Frankenstein, Zorro, and the clique might likely be awaiting my return; the barber and the shrink would undoubtedly have inquiries about what measures I had taken to alleviate their plight. Oh, dear God! The nightmare was resurfacing. I was standing on the edge of a precipice ...

"You could not have picked a more inopportune day to forget your wallet," remarked the sergeant, a sentiment I could not help but concur wholeheartedly.

"Apologies, truly apologies," I uttered, but my words fell upon deaf ears as he had already turned his attention to his fellow officers. With a curt command, he directed one of them to comb me. Oddly, Robert remained untouched, standing there in silence, observing with a detached gaze as the policeman's practised hands swiftly ransacked my clothing and delved into my pockets. My heart pounded like a relentless drumbeat, and when the officer extracted the revolver, eliciting surprised looks from his colleagues, I blushed deeply, my embarrassment akin to that of an adolescent virgin caught in the act of self-indulgence. I felt consumed by guilt, unable to meet the gaze of the policemen, and instinctively braced myself for the impending ordeal.

The policeman handed the revolver to his superior, who removed the barrel and inspected it with an experienced eye. He glanced in Robert's direction, who had regained a semblance of composure during our brief pause in the coffee shop, wiping away the traces of grease from his cheeks. He now appeared strangely calm, as if the entire situation bore no relevance to him. The sergeant then turned his attention back to me, his lips curling into a sardonic grin as he remarked:

"A gun? You were involved in the riot, were you not?"

It felt less like a question and more like an indictment, a heavy charge in the air. I stammered incoherently:

"No, no, no... There's been a mistake... an... uh... a mistake, sir."

As I faltered, he continued with biting irony:

"A mistake? The gun doesn't belong to you? Perhaps we slipped it into your pocket, sir, didn't we?"

His sarcasm cut more profound than any accusation. It was clear he had already judged and sentenced me. I couldn't help but wonder how many years I'd be facing this time.

"It's not what I meant, sir. I... uh..."

"Shut your rotten mouth, you little wretch! I'll curse your mother, your sister, your father, your entire bloody family and every damn relative! Trust me, if you utter another word, a single word, I'll have my way with you. Take him away before I commit murder!"

***

Approximately fifteen agonising minutes later, we were seated on a worn wooden bench in a grimy and squalid room at the police headquarters. Robert's spirit had been thoroughly crushed. He had vehemently protested, raised his voice, and even threatened to complain to his embassy, but his efforts had been in vain. It appeared that no one comprehended his impassioned words. Eventually, he resigned himself to the wait, recognising that there was little else we could do.

Time seemed to stretch endlessly in that room. It was barren, furnished with a solitary desk at its centre and two elongated benches. The walls bore the weight of age, their surfaces discoloured and forlorn, as if they hadn't seen a fresh coat of paint in a century. A portrait of the ubiquitous President adorned one of the walls—a constant reminder of Abdelghani's watchful gaze. Beneath the frame, a noticeboard proclaimed, "***The Police Is AT The Service Of The People***!" It was meant to be reassuring, but our current predicament felt far from comforting.

My irritation grew with each passing minute. Allowing us to languish for over an hour was far from acceptable. Robert had fallen silent, and I had nothing to offer by way of solace. I understood that it wasn't our uncertain circumstances that troubled him most but rather the inexplicable disappearance of his wife.

Two hours dragged on, and my frustration reached its breaking point. I was on the verge of raising my voice when Robert inquired, "Are they going to leave us waiting until tomorrow?"

I rose from my seat and headed towards the door, guarded by a vigilant sentinel. I intended to inquire whether I could speak with their superior, but a detective entered the room just then.

"Who's Robert Waterbird?" he inquired.

As Robert stood up, he handed him back his passport and said, "Please, have a seat."

We settled onto the same bench while the detective stood in the room's centre, his legs slightly apart, an aura of authority about him, as if he were prepared for a confrontation.

"Why were you wandering the streets at that hour, Mr. Waterbird? Were you involved in the riot?" he asked, his scepticism evident.

Robert explained our quest to locate his wife, who went shopping unaware of the demonstration, recounting how we had inadvertently become trapped in the chaotic march. The detective remained somewhat suspicious, casting a sidelong glance at me, and inquired, "You didn't need a revolver to find the lady, did you?"

There was no room for equivocation. I decided to employ a high-stakes strategy. Rather than directly answering the detective's question, I said, "You'll get a clear answer when you speak with the Director of Security. Don't forget to mention that his brother-in-law is in your custody... or perhaps, to avoid undue concern, simply inform him that he is your guest, Detective."

Brother-in-law! I was the first to be surprised by my audacity. I had never before referred to myself in such a manner, and I was not very proud at the time because of what I was told about Hassan's possible involvement in the massacre of 'Ouja. However, I had no other choice, and my stratagem worked. The detective was taken aback.

"The brother-in-law of the DS? You, sir?" he inquired, startled.

I nodded in affirmation. "Indeed, I have that honour, Detective."

A peculiar sensation, a mixture of trepidation and guilt, stirred within me. Secretly, I cursed myself for aligning with the enemy so readily.

"May I request your name, sir?" the detective asked.

"I am Bassam Bourasin," I replied.

The detective excused himself and exited. Ten anxious minutes later, he returned, slightly out of breath, bowing humbly as he spoke:

"I deeply apologise for the inconvenience, sir. I entreat you to accept our sincerest apologies. We were entirely unaware, and if only you had informed us from the outset..."

"I couldn't," I exclaimed angrily. "That blasted sergeant threatened to wreak havoc on my entire family if I dared to utter a word. Where is he now?"

The detective responded, "Well, he is...ahem! Probably patrolling the streets, sir."

"Very well," I retorted. "When he returns, advise him to exercise greater civility, as he may find himself in a precarious situation next time."

"I will not fail to convey that message, sir... um... Your chauffeur is on his way to take you back to the hotel, sir."

"Excellent! May I also request that you make inquiries to ascertain whether Mrs Waterbird has been spotted by any of your patrols?"

"Indeed, sir, we will do our utmost to locate her... unless she is already back at the hotel. I will personally oversee the matter."

I thanked the detective and strolled down the corridor with Robert to await our car at the entrance of the police headquarters. Curiosity and excitement gleamed in Robert's eyes as he inquired, "What the hell did you tell the officer? His attitude changed completely!"

"Oh, nothing extraordinary," I replied casually. "Just that I am a relative of his hierarchic superior."

He watched me with a growing curiosity and let out a chuckle.

"Really? That's quite clever!"

"It's almost true," I admitted with a smirk.

"Almost?" he laughed heartily. "Ingeniously cunning! But it worked, damn it!"

"I didn't entirely fabricate it, you know," I explained. "I do happen to have connections in the higher echelons of the security apparatus."

"Ah, well! It's always reassuring to have the right connections," he mused.

"My dear Robert, you mustn't be so unwaveringly naive, especially after everything you've witnessed and heard today; it would be unforgivable. I have no faith in the police, and my acquaintance with a high-ranking security official does not bring me any sense of comfort. Quite the opposite. They are among the least trustworthy individuals in this country. Don't make the mistake of thinking they are dedicated to their duty out of some noble allegiance, for those people possess no loyalty whatsoever. In fact, they would collaborate with His Majesty the Devil himself if he were willing to work with them. I have some insight into this matter. You can purchase a policeman's uniform for less than twenty dollars; you can acquire his firearm for a little more. And if you're feeling generous, you can access all the doors of the Ministry of the Interior. They'll welcome you with open arms and warmth if you keep paying, but be cautious! The moment you turn your back on them, you'll inevitably be stabbed. As I mentioned, I have some knowledge in this area. Two out of every four men in this country are undercover working for the police or affiliated with one or more of the security departments. They aren't in these roles because it's their calling but rather because they couldn't find any other means of making a living and particularly if they were coerced into cooperating with the enemy of the people. That's why most of the individuals involved with this business harbour animosity toward foreigners, especially if they they think them rich. My dear Robert, they dislike you because you represent a different kind of culture, a distinct system of thought, an alternative way of life, which they believe they must combat because freedom should not be allowed. You saw how they treated the students, didn't you? They weren't attempting to contain them peacefully; they were venting their frustrations. These are disillusioned men, Robert. Were they not attempting to exact revenge on the society they were supposed to protect? I admit this is the Militia's misconduct, but they are a parallel police. Let me divulge more: Our police forces serve as a sanctuary for thugs, ruffians, crooks, rapers, killers, thieves, Mafiosi, cutthroats, degenerate jerks, and other unfortunate and destitute souls. In short, it's a haven for those who have failed in other professions and continue to be welcomed by the police. So, how can you possibly expect me to be reassured simply because I know one of their chiefs?"

Robert pondered my words for a long while, his gaze fixed morosely on the damp, dimly lit street. The chilly breeze rustled our clothing and set the branches of nearby trees swaying and dancing gracefully. Above the city's towering buildings, the sky had once again cleared, unfurling its murky, star-speckled dome. A serene moon gleamed brightly, its radiance oblivious to our tumultuous escapade.

"Mr. Bassam, you seem to have forgotten your revolver," remarked the detective, who had unexpectedly joined us, extending the firearm towards me. I stared at him, momentarily taken aback, while he held out the weapon. I was on the verge of explaining that the revolver wasn't mine, but at the last moment,

I chose to accept it, avoiding the need for further explanations. Thus, I pocketed the firearm and expressed my gratitude.

***

Tomorrow, I am set to visit my bank. Surprisingly, it brings me a sense of delight, even though my life has undergone such profound changes. Hamda La'war's confession has alleviated a heavy burden that had weighed on my conscience. I had carried the weight of my mother's death and the tragedy of my fiancée as if I were the perpetrator, given my association with the man presumed to be the mastermind behind the massacre.

Upon returning to the hotel, Hassan called me and invited me to their party. I explained that I was utterly exhausted and unable to meet his sister or anyone else, offering my apologies. He seemed to understand my explanation and did not press further.

I wasted my time at the hotel the following day, perusing newspapers, jotting down notes, and consuming excessive tea and coffee. I dined with Robert, who appeared deeply perturbed by the unfolding events in the country. Later, I retired to my room and slumbered until the voice of the Muezzin stirred me at dawn.

I quickly realised that my idle existence in the city was far more tedious and disconcerting than my arduous days in 'Ouja. I had grown weary of the capital, fatigued by its ostentatious luxury and disenchanted with my current way of life. For a fleeting moment, I contemplated a permanent return to my village. However, the nagging question that held me in place was: What purpose would it serve? I had nothing and no one to return to—a void of work, family, and connection. I had been severed from 'Ouja, uprooted, and left adrift.

After lunch, I ventured out for a stroll through the bustling streets. What struck me was the sheer number of foreigners teeming in the city. The majority hailed from various parts of Asia: Indians, Pakistanis, Indonesians, Malays, etc. They were immigrants, primarily labourers drawn by the allure of quick riches offered by an oil-exporting nation. They likely arrived with grand hopes and dreams, never suspecting that, in a short time, they'd find themselves conscripted into the army, serving as mere cannon fodder in battles against the Scoundrel—or perhaps aligning with the adverse side. Refusal to comply would result in imprisonment, and no one would ever hear from them again. I had observed many of these unfortunate souls during my time in prison. Some shared harrowing tales of their ordeals. Oddly, I had never paid them the slightest heed before my incarceration. I was aware, of course, that they lived among us, as I occasionally glimpsed them at the 'Ouja market. They were expatriates leading insular lives in closed communities, akin to ghettos, seemingly harbouring enigmatic and repulsive backgrounds. The majority of the staff at the Sheraton hailed from those distant corners of Asia. They spoke a broken Arabic intermingled with English and their languages, often appeared servile, and were likely implicated in dubious dealings. Robert confided that he had been approached by servants and waiters at least eight times, seeking currency exchange or involvement in the black market. Given the legal repercussions and risk of heavy penalties, I cautioned him against getting entangled in such activities. He chuckled and assured me, "No, I haven't engaged with them. Besides, I don't carry much cash—just traveller's cheques, which aren't useful to them." It turned out my warning was apt, as most Asians I encountered in prison were drug dealers or addicts, further reinforcing my avoidance of their disreputable company. I am aware that many of those immigrant workers disdain us, whether due to our wealth compared to their poverty or certain deep-seated prejudices. The chasm between us is so vast that it's naive to believe it could ever be bridged or broken. While we may share a common faith as Muslims, some are Christians or have different beliefs. Common faith alone is insufficient to foster camaraderie. We may share a historical link with the British colonial experience, but our shared history of subjugation has only amplified our sense of isolation, much as it has for them. Arguing that we are all Third World peoples and should stand in solidarity is a political slogan. In reality, the divide between rich and poor is insurmountable. This is the world as God has ordained it; it is Mektub.

We were exceedingly destitute before discovering the vast oil reserves beneath our desert. Our fathers and forefathers endured harsh lives but were resilient and robust. They traversed long distances across barren landscapes under the relentless sun, mounted on camelbacks. Now, we cruise in Buicks, Cadillacs, Rolls-Royces, 4X4s and other fast-moving vehicles, living and working in air-conditioned comfort. Our strength and resilience remain undiminished, thanks to Allah's mercy. However, the relentless cycle of coups and counter-coups is hardly surprising. We are consumed by the thirst for power, which is far from ordinary. Every minor tribal or clan leader regards himself as a Sun God within his territory. The state is a complex web of alliances, a peculiar concoction. To an outsider looking at the city, the imperious beast remains invisible to the naked eye. Yet, beneath the tranquil metropolis's veneer, the unrest elements simmer. We are a nation in the throes of birthing, and no one truly knows what kind of offspring we nurture. This is precisely what Hamda La'war unveiled through his televised confession.

After dinner with Janet and Robert that evening, we all went to my room. Janet didn't mind having a drink with us because it was their last night in the country. So Robert brought his bottle, duly muffled as usual, inside the newspaper's sheet, and we settled in the tiny living, drinking, smoking, and chattering. At the same time, the TV blared a monotonous program. The night was lovely, and a cool breeze fluffed the muslin curtains on the balcony. Janet was dressed in a long blue gown with a dingy sheen, contrasting beautifully with her white skin. She appeared to be more attractive than ever. Her golden hair caressed her shoulders, and her blue eyes seemed so bright and clear that I was about to forget myself and tell her honestly that I was under her spell. But, at the last second, I hesitated and abstained. I wasn't sure how she'd react - maybe warmly with a welcoming smile. But what if she felt I was making an advance on her? What would a woman do in such a situation? I'm not sure because I have minimal experience with ladies. Besides, she is a foreigner, and thus, my guest and her husband were not even in the room at the time since he had gone to fetch the bottle of whisky, and when he returned, I was no longer anxious to discuss my crush. Nonetheless, my bewilderment reached an all-time high because we were no longer in the lift by that point but in my room, and even if something happened between us, I would never be able to acknowledge it.

"You should come and see us one of these days," Janet suggested.

"Thank you so much. If I travel to England, I will."

We raised our glasses.

"To friendship," Robert said.

The white stars glittered in their remote dome through the balcony, and the moonshine's reflection on the glasses added a vivid rapturousness to our reunion.

"You'll have a hard time around here," Robert said.

"Oh, you know, that won't be the first time. Anything can become habitual."

"However, the Islamists do not appear to be ready to leave very soon."

"No one wants to give up power, even if it is difficult to maintain it without killing. You witnessed what happened; some of the students were killed or incarcerated, while others were compelled to play the government's game. The city is a graveyard two days after the riot. Nobody speaks up, and no one protests. Those who go against the grain are labelled traitors. However, we did not arrive at this point because the people in power are fundamentalists; far from it. We would reach the same deadlock if the previous president was still in power. In fact, regardless of religion, our rulers are all the same. They're all made of the same stuff. Tyranny is a legacy. Our history is rife with bloodshed; we generate dictators as easily as we breed violence. If you want my honest opinion, the Arab world is doomed with or without oil."

There was a brief pause. Robert refilled our glasses. "Just a finger for me," Janet said.

"Ladies and gentlemen, our gallant security forces have finally laid their hands on the criminal who had provoked, planned, and committed the heinous massacre of 'Ouja," the TV speaker declared. That man, Hamda La'war, a prominent Scoundrel agent, is responsible for the deaths of hundreds of innocents in the village where he held the highest authority. Here's his full confession..."

The image of Hamda La'war flashed on the screen immediately. He was sitting on a chair with nothing but a white wall behind him. He wore a long robe that reached his ankles. His face looked both enraged and bloated. On his cheekbones and nose, a few dark tumescences emerged. He lacked the black patch that he used to cover his blind eye, and he appeared weary, worn, and vacuous as if he hadn't slept in two or three nights. I was more stunned than surprised and silently turned over to fix the screen as if mesmerised.

Robert became aware of my anxiousness.

"What's going on?" he questioned, peering at the TV screen.

I explained what I had just heard. Janet sighed deeply and continued, pointing to Hamda's swollen face, "He has a really horrible look."

"Hushhh... Let's listen," Robert commanded. "I got the strange impression of something already known or seen!"

***

"I am Hamda Mohammed Abderrahman, known as Hamda La'war. For nearly two decades, I held the position of president in the cell of 'Ouja. I also occupied prominent roles within the Village Council until I became mayor. However, when the revolution erupted, I was in the same position. Despite this, I made a fateful decision to flee the village, driven by the certainty that my enemies would seek vengeance for the offences I had committed against them. I was well aware that the new regime would hold many political figures accountable. My apprehensions extended not only to the new government but also to my fellow villagers. During my years of service, which spanned nearly two decades, I had amassed influence in high circles but had also garnered a multitude of enemies. When news reached me that our compatriots were assembling in the south, I hastened to join them. Subsequently, as foreign countries, whom we had previously counted as allies, were on the verge of recognizing the Islamic regime as the de facto government, we devised a plan to counter this development. We engaged mercenaries with known ties to the underworld, offering them substantial sums of money. With the assistance of some discreet allies, we facilitated their entry into the country, disguising them as tourists. I personally oversaw the entire operation, from its inception to its conclusion. Once their task was completed, the mercenaries departed for Europe while I remained in the capital, where I coordinated efforts to incite riots with certain students. We distributed firearms and financial resources to the rioters, but before I could see our plans through, I was apprehended by the police."

A voice in the studio interjected, seeking clarification:

"So, are you suggesting that both the massacre in 'Ouja and the riots in the capital were orchestrated by you and your associates, including 'The Scoundrel'?"

Hamda nodded solemnly, acknowledging the truth:

"That is precisely what transpired."

The interrogator continued:

"How did you establish contact with these mercenaries?"

"We have allies and supporters in Europe."

"Could one refer to these allies as agents?"

Hamda contemplated for a moment before responding:

"Yes, if you wish to characterize them as such."

The questions persisted:

"How did you manage the entry and exit of these mercenaries without arousing suspicion?"

"We bribed certain airport employees."

"Were they police officers or customs officials?"

"No, they were ordinary airport employees tasked with facilitating the arrival of what they believed to be a charter of European tourists."

"Why did you opt for mercenaries instead of carrying out these actions yourselves?"

A pause hung in the air, Hamda hesitating before answering:

"No one within our ranks was willing to carry out these tasks."

"Even among the rebels?"

Hamda's response was uncertain

"Yes, sir."

"Does this imply that, under certain circumstances, your rebel forces might refuse to execute orders issued by 'The Scoundrel'?"

Hamda remained ambivalent:

"I cannot say for certain... It's possible... I don't really know."

"Are there mercenaries within your ranks?"

Hamda admitted:

"Yes, perhaps around a hundred or so."

"Were they involved in the 'Ouja massacre?"

"I believe they were."

"How did they escape when your forces were surrounded?"

"The desert is vast..."

My heart raced with anticipation. I feared the imminent question: "Where were you hiding when you were apprehended?" I reached for my glass of whisky, my palms moist with anxiety. I seemed to be part of the interrogation as if my involvement might be exposed. What if Hamda publicly revealed my complicity? I had allowed him to seek refuge in my room; I was his unwitting accomplice. What an unfortunate fate! I was destined to be a willing or unwilling accomplice to a heinous act. Was this truly inevitable? If not Hassan, then Hamda! It was a wretched curse.

I reached for my handkerchief to wipe away the cold sweat trickling down my neck and temples. The interrogation pressed on:

"How did you bribe the students?"

"We didn't need to bribe everyone, just certain leaders."

"For what purpose did you do this?"

"It was for the sake of the revolution."

"Or a counter-revolution."

"Indeed, if you prefer that term. The outcome was the same."

"You mentioned that some foreigners assisted you. Can you provide specifics?"

"Well, we were encouraged by the Western world to act..."

"Are you suggesting that Western public opinion incited you to commit such heinous acts?"

"No, sir, that's not what I meant. However, they are not particularly supportive of the Islamic regime in the West."

"Even if they aren't supportive, it doesn't mean they endorse your actions, Mr. Hamda."

"Perhaps not, but many of them stand with us against you, regardless of our actions."

"Could you provide an example to clarify?"

"Well, those working for oil companies aren't all on your side, are they?"

"Are you referring to engineers and other experts? What leads you to believe that?"

Hamda hesitated again, then spoke:

"It's quite evident, really. They are Christians, and they may find it difficult to coexist with your regime..."

"We've coexisted for centuries, Mr. Hamda."

"Yes, through conflict! But they aren't pleased with a regime that restricts what they hold dear..."

"What do they hold dear?"

"Everything you prohibit: alcohol, entertainment, casinos... in essence, life."

"We're not prohibiting these things for Christians but for Muslims."

"You're curtailing people's freedoms."

"You, Mr. Hamda, are a turncoat and a traitor. Don't forget that. Furthermore, your words do not justify the massacre of three hundred innocent lives. You are the last person who should speak of freedom or anything else. You are concealing a crucial fact: these foreign experts have been coerced by 'The

Scoundrel.' They are hostages in his war, while you portray them as willing participants."

Hamda lowered his head in silence and then muttered:

"Yes, sir."

"Do you admit that they are your hostages?"

"I do."

"Did 'The Scoundrel' exert pressure on them to secure their cooperation?"

"He certainly did, sir."

"For instance?"

"Everything was employed: threats, blackmail, bribes... They are not saints. We offered them money, whisky, and women, and they were willing to do whatever was asked of them."

A moment of silence followed.

"Do you feel remorse now?"

Hamda bowed his head and spoke with a broken voice:

"Yes, sir, I do."

"Do you acknowledge your betrayal?"

"Yes. I... I am a traitor."

And so concluded this strange interview. I rose from my seat and switched off the TV. Returning to my chair, I was overwhelmed with emotion. Robert refilled my glass while Janet stared silently at the balcony. The night was eerily calm, though not reassuring or comforting. Wrapped in my sombre thoughts, I struggled to comprehend Hamda's unsettling confession. Something remained elusive in his behaviour. How could a man willingly commit such acts against his neighbours and friends? I understood that the villagers were not overly fond of him; some may have even harboured deep-seated hatred and wished for his imprisonment or death. Perhaps the feeling was mutual. However, there was a significant chasm between harbouring ill will and taking action. Hamda had crossed that line without apparent hesitation.

Nonetheless, one couldn't willingly shoulder such unforgivable charges without the possibility of having been coerced through threats of torture. Could that be the case? It seemed entirely plausible, and I mulled it over for two days and nights. But when the radio announced the beheading of Hamda La'war at dawn the next day, I abandoned that notion and thought: "It's over. We may never know the whole truth, for it likely perished with the deceased."

***

Robert and Janet, with a sense of purpose and anticipation, embarked on their homeward journey as the sun began to cast its first rays upon the horizon. I found myself in the company of my acquaintances as we embarked on a journey to the airport, nestled within the luxurious confines of my Mercedes. Yet, a sense of compunction and guilt began to pervade my being. A detached and amicable demeanour marked our parting. Robert's eyes gleamed mischievously as our hands met in a brief but firm clasp. He leaned in close, his words barely audible as he uttered, "I extend my sincerest condolences for the loss of your dear aunt." It appeared that she had endured a severe ordeal at the hands of the authorities."

I found myself withholding my breath. He smiled, his countenance betraying a hint of amusement, before proceeding with his response in a measured tone, "She, it seems, did not divulge the entirety of her secrets, did she?"

"No, she did not," I retorted. How did you come to possess such knowledge?

Ah! Never have I been deceived. The application of cosmetics was dreadfully inept!"

Upon my return to the hotel, a profound sense of solitude and despair enveloped me, compelling me to sequester myself within the confines of my room for an entire day, steadfastly declining any telephonic correspondence. I indulged in the frivolous celluloid narratives and televised serials, partaking in an inexhaustible array of cigarettes while concurrently imbibing an equivalent multitude of cups of tea and coffee. Finally, wearied and disinterested, I ascended from my seated position and ambulated towards the balcony, where I lingered for an indeterminate duration, fixating vacantly upon the urban landscape, devoid of any genuine perception.

***

Eight

As a matter of course, the misery did not endure. On the fateful day of Hamda's impending execution, Hassan called me, inquiring about my availability for an evening repast in the company of Sophia. In a concession to the query, I proffered a resolute affirmation. Therefore, as the clock struck eight that evening, my driver skillfully manoeuvred the sleek Mercedes, bringing it to a halt in front of the imposing iron gate that guarded the entrance to a splendid villa nestled on the fringes of the bustling city. As I descended from the vehicle, the nocturnal air enveloped me, imbued with the aromas of blossoms and roses wafting forth from the verdant expanse of the garden. Clad in a sapphire-hued outfit, meticulously procured for the auspicious occasion mere hours prior, I adorned my alabaster shirt with a charcoal-hued necktie. I felt Neither happy nor sad, but rather a curious anticipation stirred within me, eager to look at the woman who shall become my betrothed in a few fleeting days. Honestly, I remained oblivious to this fact in that particular instant despite harbouring a peculiar inclination of an inexplicable nature. With trepidation, I cautiously advanced towards the imposing iron gate, its large size commanding my attention. My hand reached out to engage the bell, its resonant chime echoing. Emerging from the depths of obscurity, a solitary figure ventured forth. The man inquired with the utmost civility, "Pray tell, might you be the esteemed Mr. Bassam?"

I assented with a subtle inclination of my head. He unlatched the gate, granting me passage. I traversed a protracted path adorned with marble, nestled betwixt the verdant sentinels of nature, aglow with the gentle radiance emanating from diminutive lamps. The gentleman, serving as my guide, abruptly halted his stride upon reaching a flight of stairs adjacent to the abode. He then pivoted towards my personage and uttered with measured intonation: "Sir, the entrance stands ajar, beckoning your presence."

I thanked him and ascended the steps that guided me towards a magnificent verandah. My gaze fell upon a slightly open door, and a maid, adorned in a voluminous white gown, graciously showed me into a grand living space. The room was aglow with the radiance emanating from a radiant chandelier suspended at its heart. In the dimly lit room, a solitary figure occupied an armchair, engrossed in the printed pages of a newspaper. Hassan, it was. He rose, resplendent in his cocoa-hued attire, and with a countenance of utmost affability, extended his hand in my direction. And lo, Sophia did make her entrance. From the very outset, her unadorned nature captivated me. At the same time, her tender gaze, akin to a gentle caress, bestowed a sense of tranquillity upon me. In due course, her triumvirate of progeny materialised, extending their salutations unto my personage, only to retreat to the sanctity of their respective chambers. The dinner, bereft of any captivating allure, would have languished in absolute indifference were it not for Sophia's enchanting and effervescent presence. I lacked the requisite composure to partake in solitary repast alongside Hassan at that particular juncture. Betwixt us, an abundance of enigmatic sentiments did reside, a profusion of veiled reproach rendered in silence. My confidence in him remained tentative, for his true intentions towards me remained elusive.

The dinner, however, was a great success, which surprised me. Although we didn't discuss marriage that night, Hassan called me the following day to ask if I was satisfied. In a calm and balanced way, I told him that our meal was okay but nothing special.

"I kindly ask you, dear friend, to discuss Sophia with me."

"Ah! Ah!" The exclamation escaped my lips, a sudden burst of emotion that could not be contained. "She's doing great. I'm truly impressed... Women like her are hard to find these days."

" Does her existence and our family connection, or the depth of your conviction, spark such profound contemplation in you?"

"Both," I responded, my voice laced with a tinge of satisfaction. "I find myself truly gratified."

A brief interlude ensued, followed by his utterance: "

"She feels the same way about you. She has happily agreed to marry you in her great kindness and understanding, joining your lives together in a beautiful relationship."

"Ah! Ahem! I am truly grateful for your kind words, as they have touched me deeply and filled me with a great sense of appreciation. It is an incredible honour."

The phantasmagorical visions that danced before my eyes were of such an otherworldly nature that I could scarcely comprehend their meaning. Yet, I felt an inexplicable sense of comfort and belonging in this strange and wondrous place.

Time seemed to lose all meaning as I drifted through the gossamer strands of my imagination, untethered from the mundane constraints of reality. It was as though I had stumbled upon a hidden corner of my psyche, a secret garden where the impossible became possible and the boundaries between dreaming and waking dissolved like mist in the morning sun.

"Are you ready for the holy union of marriage?" he asked.

"When will it happen? Should we anticipate it soon?"

He said urgently, "This matter needs to be dealt with quickly." In our family, we must recognise our tendency to be conservative. Visits and meetings between you and your fiancée, my dear friend, must be strictly forbidden, no matter how close you are. Unfortunately, people in society would certainly gossip and question her reputation, as she sadly has to deal with the stigma of being divorced from a previous marriage.

"I understand the subject perfectly."

"In that case, if you've both made up your minds, we'll get you married this coming weekend. Please, does that work for you?"

I was torn, caught between the conflicting pulls of choice and hesitation. I struggled to find the right words to say. Though I had expected this moment, its sudden arrival left me utterly surprised and lost for what to do next.

"Tell me, what's the reason for this relentless rush?"

He looked annoyed. I'm completely captivated by the complex fabric of people's lives and feel an irresistible pull toward it.

"Do we need to rush?"

" I have already explained everything to you. I don't like repeating myself. Are you having second thoughts?"

"Absolutely not. I am prepared, undoubtedly."

"Sounds good. I'll meet you in the evening. We can talk things over then."

And so it came to pass, with astonishing swiftness, that I found myself united in the sacred bonds of matrimony.

***

For two weeks, I stayed home, leaving only for social engagements where Sophia and her respected friends were present. Sophia's circle is large. Since our marriage, we've received countless invitations. But we haven't accepted all of them.

I was introduced to Hassan and Sophia's stepmother during our wedding. She attended the ceremony, and there was nothing unusual about her behaviour or interactions with Hassan and his sister. They call her "Mamma," and they show her great respect, even though she's younger than they are. The Indian's accusations of incest seem exaggerated and without evidence. She continues to live alone in the same large house with Hassan. It's too big for a single man, and she doesn't have other options since her parents are deceased, and her ties to her extended family are weak.

My unexpected discovery that Suleiman Mughli - who attended the wedding without being invited - is quite different from the respected figure I'd always thought of him as came as a surprise. He congratulated me and said, "I'm glad you've finally decided to join our prestigious group."

Once again, the question lingers: Am I one of them? This persistent query, much like a relentless ghost, haunts my thoughts.

We sat down for some refreshments after signing the marriage contract in the grand living quarters. Surrounded by unfamiliar faces, I thanked him, but the thought of joining their ranks made me uneasy, like a sting from a scorpion. I wanted to ask him what he meant but held back at the last moment. I first heard this phrase in prison when the guard Mahmoud asked the psychologist if I was one of them. In the presence of Suleiman Mughli, whose conviction was unshakable, I wondered if I had unwittingly joined the same group he belonged to. It's comforting to know that Mughli, on the day of my marriage, turns out to be an upright citizen with no ties to the Mafia, much like my own clean record.

Upon his departure, I shifted my gaze towards Hassan, my inquisitive nature compelling me to seek elucidation: "What did he exactly mean by that?"

My friend's idea that I joined the Mafia right after getting married didn't appeal to me. It felt exclusive and uninviting. I was also troubled by the comment, though thankfully, my spouse remained unaware of it, made by the person who spread this rumour, the Mughli.

Hassan appeared to possess an indomitable indifference. He casually dismissed my anxiety, saying, "Don't worry about it."

I spoke up strongly, expressing my firm disagreement from within.

"I confess, I'm troubled by your decision to invite that man to your sister's wedding. We all know about his connection to the criminal underworld. It's a well-known fact."

To my astonishment and profound dismay, Hassan emitted a light, almost ethereal, giggle. And with a gentle touch upon my shoulder, he leaned close to my ear, his voice a mere whisper: "He is not, I must confess, the embodiment of your preconceived notions, but rather, an individual who shares our collective identity."

My face turned fiery red, and anger raged inside me. I often find myself lost in the complex maze of confusion, struggling to free my baffled mind from the grip of ignorance. Sadly, I cannot grasp the illusive threads of comprehension. He truly takes on the respected role of an officer in the Intelligence Service. I fixed my gaze on him, my face showing my perplexity. I was ready to consider any idea except that one. Had he been making fun of me? At one time, he had acknowledged that Suleiman was a prominent figure in organised crime. This was well-known among the prisoners, echoing through the halls and cells. Had he been trying to hide Suleiman, suspecting that I knew about their secret dealings? I firmly grasped his arm and guided him towards a private corner of the living room, ensuring our conversation would stay hidden from curious listeners.

"Do you try to deceive me, Hassan? I know about the secret meeting you had at the Sheraton, where you dealt with the shady characters of the underworld."

In uttering such words, I wanted him to divulge the secrets concealed within his hand. I stood poised, prepared to engage him in a confrontation. His response, in all its perplexing intricacy, left me utterly confounded.

"No, no, it is not what you believe. I've informed you who he is. Why should I deceive my brother-in-law for a stranger's sake? I ask you to trust me. In his critical position, he's a significant figure. I promise you, I don't tell lies."

"Do you currently keep your agents detained?"

"Necessity dictated its inevitability. He had to go under-cover."

"Thus, one must surmise that the tale of his affiliation with the Mafia was nought but a fabrication?"

"In his current occupation, he dedicates himself diligently to the service of the State. That's an operation conducted with utmost secrecy and discretion."

My suspicions remained unabated.

"Regarding his illegal drug business, I personally saw it unfold."

"Such is the nature of existence, my dear brother-in-law."

"And what of his association with the Afghan?"

"Planned by the clandestine machinations of the Secret Service, a stratagem was devised to surreptitiously penetrate the inner sanctums of various factions."

"When I contemplated these assemblages, I was under the impression that they were aligned with your esteemed presence, or rather, in consonance with the nascent authority of the new regime."

"In our life, a profound sense of scepticism pervades our consciousness, as we've lost trust in the inherent kindness of others."

"Do you know, at least, that the Afghan is secretly plotting against you?"

Never before had I engaged in such unreserved discourse with him. He inclined his head in a gesture of understanding and responded with a measured tone, "Indeed, I'm well aware of the issue at hand. Mughli shared a detailed explanation of everything that transpired for me. I'm also aware of their attempt to hire you when you went to 'Ouja after the death of your mother and fiancee."

"Yes," I uttered, a tinge of astonishment colouring my voice. How did you come to possess such information?"

"The incarcerated Indian, weighed down by the heaviness of his wrongdoings, has confessed all of his crimes to ease his conscience."

"And what of the Afghan?"

"After the lamentable failure of the riots, he, with a heart heavy with trepidation, managed to elude the authorities' clutches, yet unfortunately for him, a number of his loyal comrades were apprehended, their fates now hanging precariously in the balance. They shall indeed face the crucible of trial."

In the recesses of my memory, I summoned the recollection of Robert's clandestine revelation regarding the complicity of the Militia in the tumultuous upheaval that had gripped the streets.

"Do they genuinely connect with those who initiated the situation?"

"They had meticulously organised everything."

I kept moving from one amazement to another, constantly thrown off balance by this never-ending sequence of surprises.

"If the Afghan really caused the riots, Hamda La'war made a bold confession on TV, but it was a false one. Who took responsibility for the chaos in these tumultuous events?"

A moment of silence ensued.

"The Afghan designed schemes to get me ousted, aiming for the Director of Security role himself. His drive for this position showcases his ambition."

"Do you mean, then, that Hamda was innately innocent?"

"No, one mustn't assume complete innocence or ignorance about the riots. Instead, his focus was on the carefully planned massacre of Ouja. As the Scoundrel's executive agent, he stood among other conspirators, now all in the hands of the law."

"Indeed?"

"Confirmed: a pair had come into our possession. In the world of TV deceit, Hamda skillfully crafted a web of lies. However, it's important to mention, his dishonesty did not involve dealings with law enforcement. He struggled to carry it out. Now, stripped bare, the Deceiver is revealed, prepared for his dishonest schemes to be exposed to the discerning public. Much anticipation builds for the upcoming confrontation with a formidable challenge."

"Could you please explain to me why Hamda was put to death before the interrogation? I need to know. Why is it necessary for him to give up his life before the thorough investigation?"

Hassan paused to let his thoughts roam free in his mind.

"I feel lacking in knowledge," he uttered, his voice trailing into the silence that followed.

I find myself traversing the vast expanse of my thoughts, contemplating the intricacies of existence. I find myself in a state of perpetual anticipation, yearning for the commencement of the trial that shall bring forth those individuals who bear the burden of my mother's and my beloved fiancée's lifeblood, intermingled with that of countless others, a crimson stain indelibly marking their very hands.

***

On this auspicious day, October the fifth, I find myself immersed in the ebb and flow of existence. The world around me pulsates with quiet energy like tranquil currents, whispering ancient secrets to those who dare listen closely. Each element weaves an intricate tapestry of life, harbouring mysteries that await discovery.

An undeniable air of conspicuousness marked the moment of my arrival at the bank. It was true. I abstained from driving my Mercedes or Zerga, instead opting for the elegant Lancia of Sophia. The Ministry of the Interior had withdrawn the car and its driver. No longer am I a guest of the State, but rather a citizen akin to the multitude... Almost, but not quite there!

I had placed my old Zerga in the garage, hoping a buyer would appear soon. The Lancia radiates energy and desire for speed with its bright red colour. I enjoy driving it around town. As usual, Sophia refuses to get behind the wheel. But, considering my new responsibility to take on her husband's role, she thinks it's appropriate that I buy a new car, drawing us even closer. When I shared my concern about buying such an expensive automobile, knowing my reliable Zerga was still mine, her response was quick and sharp: "My dear husband, do you genuinely believe I would ride on those roads in that rusty pile of metal?"

I was suddenly startled. My awareness jolted like a battery being switched on. At a pivotal moment in my life, I listened as my second partner voiced her disapproval, mirroring the exact words my first had spoken about my beloved Zerga. The weight of their disapproval left me powerless. If Zerga had been a woman, my thoughts would have turned to deception, a secret plan to separate her from me. I protested, insisting that I couldn't buy a new car. With a kind expression, she offered, "I'll buy it for you."

"I can't accept that idea."

"Why not?" she asked, her voice tinged with curiosity and scepticism.

"Well, it's an unpleasant situation for a gentleman."

We had a short but lively discussion, and I gave in. In the bigger picture, the car is for our shared use, even if she doesn't drive. I discovered I could buy it, but I used all my funds for my ambitious and significant plans instead.

I was at the bank, feeling cheerful and lighthearted. As I traversed the winding road, a sense of self-congratulation enveloped me. The formidable Capital, which had once instilled a profound sense of trepidation in me, had now lost its status as a formidable adversary worthy of my struggle. A deep understanding of self-possession and triumph welled in the depths of my being. Without uncertainty, I harboured the utmost conviction that I was destined to engage in consequential transactions. In the coming years, I shall be able to establish my financial institution. Why not, indeed? By this juncture, I am blessed with a more significant number of opportunities to realise the aspirations of yesteryear. I am already enveloped within the intricate layers of John Law's persona. I engage in a captivating dance with vast sums, where fortunes are wagered and won or lost in the blink of an eye. I find myself the object of envious and admiring gazes as countless individuals, perhaps even millions, yearn and hope for me to fulfil their desires, akin to a sorcerer, bestowing upon them wealth and prosperity. In this moment of introspection, I am pondering the possibility that I may possess an inherent inclination towards commerce. In the essence of my being, there is a river of wealth. In the realm of slumber, a recurring vision unfolds before me: a tapestry of dreams wherein mounds upon mounds of Dollars, Sterlings, Yens, Marks, Euros, RMBs and various other currencies, both familiar and obscure, amass within the confines of my sleeping chamber. They cascade into my pockets, intermingle with my books, infiltrate my notes, and even the sockets and boots that adorn my person. This deluge of wealth engulfs my surroundings, threatening to subdue me beneath its formidable weight. Curiously, the selfsame reverie has recurred numerous times since the solemnisation of my marital union. On two or three occasions, I found myself roused from slumber, my breath stifling as if smothered beneath a weighty mound of currency. In truth, it is a death of exquisite allure that any humble bank clerk would covet; yet, I find myself unable to summon the resolve to embrace such a fate. When I imparted the ethereal vision to Sophia, she pondered momentarily before uttering: "Truly, you are obliged."

"No, I am not," I replied, the voice tinged with a hint of resignation.

"You are," she insisted, resolute, "even if your awareness eludes you. One is compelled to discharge their debts or bestow alms upon the charitable organisations. If you fail to do so, you shall perish, akin to a wretched misanthrope entombed beneath an extra abundance of wealth that holds no value or purpose for your existence. My dear husband, I must tell you the tale of a forewarning dream that has befallen me."

I was perplexed, for while I possess no recollection of any outstanding debts, I am acutely aware that, akin to the characters Hassan and Mamduh, I have clandestinely appropriated a sum that does not rightfully belong to me. In brief, I found myself burdened with compunction and seized by a foreboding significance of the dream. Nevertheless, I refused to succumb to the weighty burden of guilt, persistently murmuring to myself: 'I had presumed that the State was indebted to me, if not in greater measure.' In any case, I should find myself indebted to them rather than the inverse. I shall discharge my indebtedness at the earliest opportunity that presents itself to me. I am not in opposition to the State nor the government, for I am dutifully engaged in their service. Loyalty had forever coursed through my veins, an unwavering current that defined my very being. In my dreams, would be a clearer way to express the idea. Fidelity remains my steadfast companion. I possess a canine protagonist, an entity of which I am exceedingly proud. I, in truth, am nought but their canine companion. The resonant echoes of laughter reverberated through the air, a cacophony of mirth that seemed to stretch on indefinitely.

With a buoyant spirit, I ventured into the bank's hallowed halls. Mr. Khalil warmly received me. With a calm voice, he leaned in. Before summoning the butler to guide me to my designated workspace, he said, "Mr. Bassam, our enterprise thrives with resounding success."

Indeed, one must express astonishment at such a statement. He said, " I extend my congratulations to you, for you have achieved a commendable feat. Due to our unparalleled excellence, we are deemed the preeminent financial institution within the confines of this nation. We, in our supreme competence, stand unrivalled." He interjected briskly yet courteously: "Indeed, sir, that is not the essence of my intention. I was engaged in discourse concerning the affairs that pertain to us, do you understand? The proclamation resounded with fervour, echoing through the air and reverberating within the depths of their..." He made a sweeping motion with both hands, emphasising the exclusive nature of our shared concern.

"Is it truly ours? Ah! Ah! You mean... "

A sly grin played upon his lips as he acquiesced with a subtle nod.

"Indeed, without a doubt! I discerned, sir, that the administration had approved."

"Might I be granted the privilege of mending the revered 'Ouja bank?"

"They shall," he said, his voice tinged with a subtle blend of certainty and resignation. He halted, his thoughts momentarily arrested, before interjecting with a tinge of apprehension, "Regrettably, there exists a minor stipulation, I must confess."

"Yes, pray tell, what is the nature of your inquiry?"

He maintained a profound silence, his countenance betraying the weight of contemplation as though he were profoundly introspecting the circumstances.

"Well, I would prefer to disclose it to you. The project, it seems, shall not be bestowed upon a mere bank employee."

"Ah! Why not?" I asked, my tone carrying a mix of curiosity and defiance. The question hung in the air, pregnant.

"The irregularity of it, sir, is quite evident. In our establishment, it is strictly forbidden for our esteemed employees to engage in pecuniary transactions with their own financial institutions, thereby precluding any possibility of reaping personal gains from their respectable positions. This is nothing short of a manifestation of nepotism!"

A profound sense of disillusionment overcame me.

"Ah, alas, they fail to understand, Mr. Khalil. The pecuniary gains that may accrue from this enterprise have little consequence for me. Instead, my feelings are driven by sentimentality. I previously conveyed to you the profound emotional bond I forged with the esteemed financial institution, Ouja Bank. This story includes all of my youthful days, life experiences, and professional achievements up to now."

"I apprehend your meaning with utmost clarity," he rejoined.

A moment of stillness ensued as he seemed entirely absorbed. As I prepared to bid him farewell, he uttered these words: "I have pondered upon this matter in the preceding days. I perceive nought as a solitary quandary that portends specific perils."

I hurriedly expressed: "I am prepared to embark upon venturesome endeavours."

"In that case, it would be prudent for you to tender your resignation from the esteemed banking institution."

"Could I please ask for your forgiveness for my presumptuousness?"

"It is but a trifling formality, Mr Bassam, yet it bears great significance. Should you relinquish your position, rest assured that no impediments shall be placed in your path, for it is evident that you are one of our own, do you get it?"

In a moment of profound revelation, I confronted the stark realisation that my affiliation with the collective, the essence of being "one of them," could potentially serve as a formidable impediment to my path towards professional advancement. In an instant, it seized my attention. I found myself in a state of profound bewilderment.

Finally, I uttered with a heavy heart, "I must express my deepest remorse, Mr. Khalil. Indeed, one finds oneself confronted with a thorny predicament. The crux of the matter lies in the precarious dilemma that shall befall me should I choose to tender my resignation from the esteemed institution of banking. In one fell swoop, I shall be bereft of the well-deserved emoluments that have accrued to me over the course of a decade and a half, not to mention the forfeiture of my monthly remuneration and the promising prospects of my nascent position. Moreover, I find myself bereft of any assurance whatsoever that my voluntary relinquishment would inevitably result in the acquisition of said agreement."

"I assure you, Mr. Bassam, that my word is steadfast and unwavering. With your gracious concession of a just interest, I am confident in my ability to navigate this affair deftly. Nonetheless, your resignation assumes a formality that is as essential as expected. It does not necessarily entail the forfeiture of your privileges as a longstanding employee of the esteemed bank. It is but a fleeting acquiescence, a charade, designed to demonstrate that during your acquisition of the enterprise, you were not gainfully engaged within the confines of the financial institution. Do you get my point, dear colleague?"

"Do you imply that my labour shall persist unabated?"

"There shall be no need for you to desist, sir. You shall persist in your customary labour whilst concurrently proffering unto me a retroactively penned letter of resignation, encompassing the duration of your sojourn within... within..."

"Jail?"

And so it was, the culmination of all that had come before. The moment had arrived, unassuming yet pregnant with significance.

"Exactly. Thus, rather than stating that you were confined

within the walls of a prison, we shall express that you had willingly relinquished your freedom. Verily, we shall not remunerate thee for the temporal expanse encompassing thy voluntary departure, a span of approximately half a year, perchance even shorter... We shall regard it as an unpaid respite, a matter of legality. During that period, you found yourself in solitude, from which you procured the advantageous deal. Upon the conclusion of your sojourn and your subsequent reintegration into the realm of duty, it must be noted that we, in no manner, sought to subvert the established order or transgress the boundaries imposed upon us. You, in fact, were not counted among our esteemed cadre of employees at the time of your fortuitous transaction, for we had yet to commence the disbursement of a customary remuneration to you. The actions you undertook at that moment and how you executed them lie solely within your preoccupation. Thus far, our pursuit remains within the bounds of legality. Do you possess the capacity to fathom the depths of my being? What are your ruminations on this particular stratagem?"

A profound sense of awe enveloped my contemplation, rendering me speechless. Never had I fathomed the depths of Mr. Khalil's cunning and intellect.

"I must express my admiration, sir," I ventured, "for your astute stratagem. It is indeed a testament to your intellectual prowess."

A mirthful chuckle escaped him, his fingers delicately caressing the knot of his tie. At the same time, a coughing fit ensued, perhaps due to an overwhelming abundance of delight, as I surmised. I perceived his countenance to be adorned with an air of exultation, evidently gratified by the compliment I had bestowed upon him. He assumed an air of slight haughtiness as he unveiled the contents of a drawer within his desk, revealing a pristine sheet of paper which he graciously extended towards me.

"Mr. Bassam, I have meticulously prepared everything, as I trusted in your inherent wisdom. This document, dear colleague, bears witness to your voluntary departure from our esteemed institution. Naturally, it has been meticulously prepared in advance and adheres to the customary formalities. It is, but your signature is required, my dear colleague."

I accepted the document, perused its contents, and affixed my signature. And so, he unfurled yet another sheet as if unveiling a hidden treasure.

"Kindly peruse this document and affix your signature to it."

On the auspicious occasion of October the first, the paper conveyed the momentous news of my ascension to the esteemed position of chief of the department of transfer and exchange. Without a shred of uncertainty, it was abundantly clear that my ascension in rank intimately correlated with the sacred bond of matrimony I had recently entered into. The esteemed sibling of the Director of Security, undoubtedly deserving of a modest token from the reputable financial institution from whence her betrothed's elevation was procured. Nevertheless, I found myself earning such a fate, having spent a gruelling fifteen years toiling away as a lowly clerk in our humble outpost of 'Ouja. And so it was that I affixed my signature upon the legal paper, that sacred document which held the weight of my fate within its fibres. With a sense of solemnity, I relinquished it into the hands of Khalil, that enigmatic figure who stood before me, his countenance a reflection of the mysteries hidden within his soul.

Subsequently, I ascended to my nascent office on the tertiary level of the grand edifice, wherein I tarried until the meridian hour, perusing periodicals and gazettes, imbibing the elixirs of coffee and tea, and indulging in the vice of tobacco. There remained but a scant measure of labour to be undertaken. In all candour, there existed a need for more activities, for the remaining staff members launched the entire work. Shortly before midday, Sophia called me to inquire about the latest appointment. I conveyed to her my profound contentment. Her countenance mirrored my own satisfaction. All seemed to be in order. At long last, the dolce vita had deigned to commence.

***

In that very week, I saw fit to disseminate an announcement through the esteemed pages of the local periodicals, heralding the arrival of the illustrious 'Bourasin Company of Construction'. In response to the advertisement, I engaged the services of the Asiatic labourers. Through Sophia's resourcefulness, I received a loan graciously granted by the esteemed institution of the bank. As fate would have it, the very same financial institution has taken me under its employ, forging a bond of an intimate professional association. The loan, alas, bore her name. I secured a modest abode within the confines of the Sheraton. This dwelling would soon transform into the esteemed establishment 'Bourasin Company'. It comprises a pair of rooms, a kitchenette and a lavatory situated on the ground floor of the establishment. Though it may be slightly extravagant, it is a pragmatic choice, for in our line of work, the veneer of things holds utmost significance. In my capacity, I would have readily procured a humble studio within the urban confines for the very same objective; however, Sophia vehemently emphasised that those who engage with us would form their judgements based on superficial appearances. I acquiesced with a certain measure of willingness to her desire, albeit not without a tinge of reluctance, for I harboured a suspicion that Mr Ali, the astute manager of the esteemed Sheraton establishment, would seize this opportune moment to resurrect the memories I so fervently sought to repress.

I realised that I was mistaken. The moment our signatures graced the contract, he assumed a sycophantic demeanour. He uttered with feigned humility, "Might I be so bold as to inquire whether your noble solicitude for the destitute denizens of the Medina ought to be incorporated within the ambit of our financial disbursements?"

The utter lack of tact and the constant irritation were indistinguishable in their audacity. I retorted, "Mr. Ali, I am acutely cognizant of the predicament that plagues them. For this very reason, I find myself establishing an entire enterprise dedicated to the art of construction. Did I not do better?"

He offered his apologies, his words tapering off into silence. From that fateful day, he abstained from alluding to my erstwhile commitment, nevermore.

I decorated the space with two writing desks, an opulent mahogany for my personal use, and a significantly humbler counterpart for my diligent secretary. I acquired a collection of seating apparatuses in commerce, including chairs, armchairs, and a luxurious canapé. Furthermore, I procured a computing device, which I affectionately christened Samir II, as a token of appreciation for its predecessor, Samir I, who faithfully served as my steadfast companion during my tenure at the esteemed 'Ouja Bank. I affixed a modest plaque upon the door, denoting the essence and intent of this office. One finds great pleasure in perusing the inscription upon the gate, wherein the enchanting words "Bourasin Company Of Construction" are elegantly inscribed. However, this mere progression represents a solitary stride; the subsequent endeavour shall entail the audacious pursuit of Bourasin Bank! Ah! Thus do I yearn, for such is my desire, inshallah! In the echoes of my mother's wisdom, she often proclaimed, "Everything is Mektub." And now, as I cast my gaze upon the written word, I discern with great clarity: Bourasin Company Of Construction, meticulously inscribed upon the door, its message accessible to all who dare to read the Mektub!

The formidable quandary lay in the persona of the secretary. Instinctively, I yearned for a woman of refined sensibilities to preside over my telephonic correspondences, meticulously orchestrate my agenda, and attend to the intricacies of my commercial affairs. However, Sophia harboured a dissenting viewpoint. She opined that the fairer sex is ill-suited for such a formidable occupation, which necessitates the secretary's intimate engagement with the labourers, most of whom hail from foreign lands. Moreover, within the confines of an Islamic nation, the notion of women engaging in labour alongside their male counterparts remains an impermissible proposition. I conveyed to her the prevailing circumstance at the bank, wherein the fairer sex continues to toil alongside us diligently, their presence undiminished, their dwellings shared in equal measure. With a tone of detachment, she uttered, "It bears an air of dissimilarity," and appended, "Nevertheless, it shall not endure, regardless!" Once more, I acquiesced to the demands of the situation and engaged the services of a gentleman to fulfil the task at hand. Hassan directed him towards my humble office upon my desire for companionship. Khalifa, a robust gentleman of middle age, possesses a countenance adorned with luxuriant eyebrows, a receding hairline, and a determined jawline. I assented to his presence, for it was upon the assurance of my brother-in-law that his trustworthiness had been established. When I inquired of him, he vehemently refuted any association with the esteemed constabulary or affiliation with the honourable Ministry of the Interior. I harboured an unwavering conviction that his words were but a tapestry of deceit. However, should he prove to be Hassan's undercover agent, as my intuition suggests, I find myself mainly indifferent to this revelation. I possess no secrets to veil.

Furthermore, I intend to maintain an impeccable standard in my dealings, just as I have always done in the bustling streets of 'Ouja. I shall abstain from engaging the services of foreign labourers whose documentation fails to meet the requisite regularity standards. I shall be willing to part with a more significant sum, provided that tranquilly shall be bestowed upon me in return. In my unyielding manner, I have criticised numerous labourers upon that very terrain, urging them to enlist in the military or elucidate their circumstances with utmost clarity.

The matter of recruiting foreign labourers into our military ranks strikes me as somewhat incongruous, I must say. Moreover, one must question the inherent generosity of our actions. The arrival of these individuals to our nation can be attributed to the unfortunate circumstances of unemployment or meagre wages in their homelands. However, it is disheartening to acknowledge that we no longer represent a beacon of hope for them. Instead, we subject them to the peculiar occupation of war, which offers them little solace or prospects. I have been informed that many of them have met their untimely demise or suffered grievous wounds unless they are subjected to the captivity of the Scoundrel. These wretched souls, trapped in the depths of destitution and despair! In a state of perpetual discontent, neither finding solace within the confines of my office nor amidst the unfamiliarity of a foreign terrain, I am left adrift, suspended between two worlds, bereft of true belonging. Indeed, it is undeniable that we find ourselves compelled to safeguard our existence. In his cunning, the Scoundrel employs extrinsic soldiers of fortune to engage us in battle; in response, we also use these foreign labourers for a similar objective. The semblance of the stratagem may deceive, yet it diverges significantly, for our labouring soldiers are not akin to seasoned canines of war. Different from the mercenaries of the Scoundrel, these individuals had not undergone the rigorous training of combat across multiple battlefields before enlisting in our esteemed ranks. In executing their duties, they assume the role of a soldier with the same meticulousness and dedication as that of a mason, mechanic, plumber, cook, or any other vocation. Should they manage to evade the clutches of death or the shackles of captivity, these individuals, through the crucible of adversity, shall acquire novel proficiencies, thereby potentially securing an enduring residency within the confines of our nation's borders long after the wild storm of war has subsided. They may find themselves adorned with the accolades of war, a significant reward. Thus, upon their return to their humble abode, they shall find solace in the pride that swells within them, borne from their valiant exploits upon foreign shores. We fashioned them into gladiators of the contemporary era, these individuals who would become the heroes of eternity!

In due course, those who abstain from battle - or those with a lesser inclination towards heroism - have become employed under my auspices. Yesterday, I dispatched them to 'Ouja. I had acquired a dilapidated truck, a relic of a bygone era, with the noble intention of facilitating the arduous task of transporting men and materials. The tumultuous repercussions that ensued from that affair were indeed bewildering! In all honesty, I must express my sentiments without reservation. Until now, my sole occupation consisted of settling the debts... I remain trapped in the relentless grip of financial obligations, burdened by ceaseless payments. Verily, a pact was forged between the bank and me a mere fortnight following my discourse with Khalil. A clever and cunning fox, that animal! As I sat in my office on the third landing, patiently awaiting his arrival, he deftly and expeditiously convinced the bank of Bassam Bourasin's status as an independent entrepreneur. To my surprise, the negotiations did not stretch interminably nor burden me with the monotonous boredom I had anticipated. Contrarily, the affair flowed with a tranquil grace akin to a pristine and translucent brook from its very fount. He orchestrated the entire experience with the board. He arrived at my office, brimming with exultation, brandishing the papers in his grasp.

"This is the crucial document that connects us. It represents the highest achievement one can obtain. To whom should we express our appreciation?"

I rose to my feet, offering hospitality towards his arrival.

"Naturally, it is you, Mr. Khalil. Congratulations are in order for you! I believe you're perfectly suited to this role. It's truly impressive to find someone in this position. My sincerest appreciation goes to you, a thousand times over."

"This task wasn't easy, I assure you. But now, everything has been fixed. Let's celebrate this successful outcome with some drinks. Yes, this is indeed a happy occasion."

He carelessly flung the papers upon the desk, their weighty presence demanding my attention. Summoning the butler, we asked him to procure libations for our thirsty palates. Meanwhile, I perused the document, meticulously scrutinising the sheets and their identical counterparts, ensuring every iota of the contract was aligned. In the aftermath, I extended my hand towards Khalil, our fingers intertwining in a gesture of mutual accord. The act of signing preceding our handshake remains a detail that eludes my memory's grasp. In any case, the outcome remains indistinguishable insofar as my perspective is concerned.

"I will begin this task right away. In just three lunar cycles, our offices in Ouja will be transformed and look more beautiful. You might have witnessed an unfortunate incident if you had been there earlier. A lamentable carnage!"

He gently swayed his head, a subtle gesture of denial.

"Apologies! I admit, sir, I haven't received this honour yet."

"Ah! Mr. Khalil, you have noticed every detail. It would be prudent for you to witness its restoration and adornment."

At that moment, we quickly drank our drinks. He then said goodbye to me, wishing me luck before leaving. With his departure, I deftly concealed the replicated document of our agreement, tucking it away discreetly within the recesses of my pocket. Subsequently, I surreptitiously trailed in his wake, traversing the corridor with a calculated stealth. Given that my salary is assured, I do not need to prolong my presence within the confines of the office. It mattered not a whit whether I graced the confines of my office or not, for as the esteemed overseer of this department, my presence held no sway.

Naturally, as the master of this realm, my duties were a mere illusion, for my loyal underlings dutifully executed the laborious tasks. In any case, should any fragments of my service be enticed by the allure of idle chatter or seek to circumvent my authority, their endeavours shall be swiftly thwarted upon reaching the confines of Mr. Khalil's office. The latter shall pretend to lend an ear to their grievance only to respond: "Very well, I shall attend to the matter." And so it shall be, the affair shall meet its demise, a quiet and calculated death within the confines of his office. Who would dare to circumvent Khalil, to disturb the Chairman or his esteemed deputy with such trivial and foolish rumours?

***

Nine

On the first day of November, a significant date in the calendar, we are in Ramadan. The air is thick with anticipation as the faithful embark on a spiritual journey of self-reflection and devotion.

Since the day I entered into matrimony with Sophia, I have chanced upon a revelation of such profound magnitude that it has left an indelible mark upon my consciousness. She had convinced me that, to equip myself adequately for a statesman's captivating vocation, I needed to partake in the observance of Friday prayers at the grand mosque. By doing so, she assured me, my profound devotion to religion would be unmistakably evident, seamlessly intertwining with my unwavering allegiance to the regime. Thus, I find myself engaged in prayer, a public display of devotion incumbent upon every faithful adherent of the Islamic faith. In my observations, I have discerned that many State personnel, including those of esteemed stature, regularly attend a particular mosque. This revelation has ignited a renewed enthusiasm to exhibit greater piety towards Allah, His Prophet, and President Abdelghani, widely acknowledged as their earthly representative. In my contemplations, I have conceived a notion to embark on a sacred journey to the holy city of Mecca, accompanied by Sophia, once our financial means permit such an endeavour. Occasionally, we engage in discourse regarding this matter; henceforth, upon our return, we shall be bestowed with the honorifics of the Haj and the Hajja (for the wife), basking in a distinct form of eminence adorned with its splendid grandeur.

On this auspicious day, the seventh in the sacred month of Ramadhan, I am immersed in contemplation. The air is heavy with anticipation as the faithful devote themselves to fasting and prayer. The world seems to hold its breath, awaiting the arrival of the blessed Eid. The streets are adorned with vibrant decorations, a testament to the devotion and piety permeating believers' hearts. As the sun sets, casting a warm glow upon the city, we end our fast. In the wake of a bountiful repast, it has become my custom to traverse the path towards the mosque, where I engage in fervent prayer and immerse myself in the sacred verses of the Koran. Sophia's offspring had embarked upon a voyage to the land of America in the preceding month. The presence of the two youngsters, confined within the walls of a secondary educational institution, eludes my discerning gaze. They arrive fleetingly, these visitors, on the brief occasions of weekends and holidays. In this vast home, I live in near solitude, accompanied solely by Sophia, the maid from Pakistan, and the gardener.

I find myself in the throes of a most wretched affliction, a hangover of the most formidable nature. I am perplexed, unsure of the purpose behind these musings that shall forever remain concealed, destined to be perused by none. My ambition to chronicle the annals of the Islamic Revolution remains steadfast, unyielding to the passage of time. Perhaps, in twenty years hence, when this tumultuous medley has reached its denouement, I am inclined towards such a course of action. I am alone, for my dear companion Sophia has ventured into commerce, seeking to procure various necessities. Confined within the chamber's embrace, I am indulging in smoking with the fervour of an inebriated fireman. With a heavy heart, I feel compelled to confess that I am nought but a lowly swine devoid of any redeeming qualities or noble aspirations. On this day, I was unburdened by the rigours of fasting.

In the wake of my nocturnal transgressions, it becomes abundantly clear that such actions were entirely unnecessary. May Allah grant the Minister of the Interior forgiveness, for he bears the burden of my afflictions. Should I find myself in this present state of renegade and apostate, facing the imminent expulsion from paradise, compelled to relinquish my cherished Houri and the opulent palace that awaits me beyond, it is undoubtedly a consequence of his own doing. Honestly, the mercy of Allah knows no bounds, permeating every corner of existence. He possesses an intimate knowledge of the true orchestrator behind this chaotic predicament. He might inflict punishment on me instead, yet what infernal consequence! Should I find myself subjected to the agonising torments of the infernal realm, the bastard called Mamduh, that formidable figure of authority, renowned and esteemed Minister, the devout adherent of Islam, the unwavering politician, shall assuredly endure the searing fires of damnation for the duration of his eternal existence, and beyond. The fault that plagues him is unpardonable: a man of falsehood and hypocrisy, ensnaring not only our people but all who cross his path. Yet, more grievous still is the sin he has led me to commit in this sacred month after I had diligently sought repentance for all transgressions and readied myself for the imminent pilgrimage.

In the waning hours of twilight, Sophia was caught by an ailment, a common human illness. The tendrils of a cold had stealthily infiltrated her delicate frame, leaving her weakened and vulnerable. Succumbing to the whims of her weakened state, she surrendered to the embrace of slumber, bidding fare-well to the world earlier than her customary hour. I'm puzzled by the unusual preference for our TV shows, which, without fail, select the holy month of Ramadan to inundate us with the spectacle of belly dancing and other vapid entertainment year after year. The wretchedness of it all is simply unbearable! In-evitably, I have no complaints about belly dance as an art form, provided it is executed with finesse and grace. However, during the sacred period of Ramadan, it becomes an inconvenience, a vice, and an indulgence of excess. I disengaged the television's flickering screen and proceeded towards the culinary realm of my abode. I made the firm decision to partake in sustenance before succumbing to slumber. I, too, found myself consumed by an insatiable thirst, prompting me to embark upon a quest within the confines of my refrigerator in pursuit of a refreshing elixir to quench my longing. To my astonishment and chagrin, I discovered an absence of libations, replaced by a meagre as-sortment of milk bottles. In her customary manner, the maid indulged in a brief respite within the confines of her chamber, contrary to her usual practice of retiring only after ensuring our presence within our own sleeping quarters. I resolved against unsettling her, for she appeared to be tired. In the recesses of my mind, I was aware of a cellar hidden beneath the kitchen area, a sanctum where sustenance was meticulously preserved and stored. Amid our nation's strife, the spectre of deprivation ceaselessly prowls, casting its ominous shadow upon us, a constant presence that haunts our collective consciousness. Henceforth, we procure copious amounts of food, diligently hoarding it in a state of utmost vigilance.

Never before had I descended into the depths of the cellar, where the door unveiled itself directly within the confines of the kitchen. I endeavoured to grasp the knob, yet the gate appeared resolutely sealed. I meandered aimlessly through the culinary domain, my senses attuned to the elusive key that could unlock the mysteries of my quest. My gaze fell upon a drawer, beckoning me to explore its contents in a place bereft of any visible sign. With a sense of solace, I discovered a cluster of keys, each possessing a unique character. Methodically, I endeavoured to unlock the accursed door, testing each legend with unwavering patience. At long last, my endeavours bore fruit. As the door creaked open, my eyes beheld a seemingly interminable staircase, its steps disappearing into the abyss of darkness below. With a flick of the switch, I summoned forth the illumination and thus commenced my descent into the infernal depths. In truth, the netherworld lay in wait for my arrival, and may the divine absolve me, akin to a fiery abyss. It excelled in mimicking the celestial realm, rendering it an unparalleled paradise.

Ah, whether it be the fiery depths of hell or the blissful realms of paradise, the consequences, if indeed there are any, have now come to fruition!

Upon my descent, I found myself in profound bewilderment, casting my eyes in utter speechlessness. The underground chamber, stretching from its depths to the lofty expanse above, lay ensconced in an inundation of countless rows of glass vessels. In a corner, amidst a jumble of provisions, lay a stock-pile of sustenance: cans of preserved meat and fish, stacked high alongside sacks of sugar, flour, semolina, and an assortment of bottles containing milk, fruit juices, mineral water, and the like... The locale appeared to be an enclave teeming with an inexhaustible multitude of spirits, libations, and an extensive assortment of wines. Overwhelmed and taken aback by the serendipitous revelation, I cautiously began my enchanting exploration.

I saw a myriad forms of distinguished brands: Whisky, Gin, Rum, Brandy, Cognac, Sherry, Ricard, Berger, Port, Vodka, Champagne, Bordeaux... A symphony of libations, each with its own tale to tell. Wines hailing from the vineyards of France, the enchanting regions of Italy; Beers crafted with precision in the heartlands of Germany, the artistry of Belgium; spirits that whisper secrets from the distant lands of China and Japan... A cornucopia of intoxicating elixirs, beckoning the senses with their diverse origins and flavours. And an innumerable array of libations from lands I had never fathomed the possibility of beholding. Not only did the collection loom vast and opulent, but it stood as the very embodiment of Dionysos himself.

It goes without saying that after that initial instance of astonishment, I found myself in utter madness. In the depths of my ruminations, I found solace in the notion that this must be the triumph of my wife's erstwhile consort. Whether it slipped his memory upon his departure from this abode, or he underwent a profound transformation, embracing piety and severing all ties with the possessions he entrusted to Sophia's care, with the fervent wish that she would not hesitate to obliterate them. However, inexplicably, she refrained from doing so. Her silence on the matter led me to surmise that she had either carelessly overlooked it or was covertly attempting to deliver it to an undisclosed foreign purchaser clandestinely; such a revelation would not astonish me, as Sophia possesses an impeccable acumen for business. At that moment, I resolved to partake in a mere sip of the Brandy, if only to ascertain that the entirety of its contents was not a deceitful fabrication intended to beguile not only myself but any unsuspecting soul. My curiosity was piqued, for my eyes were yet to comprehend the scene before me fully. I yearned for concrete evidence to solidify my wavering belief. After completing my forthcoming activities, I shall partake in a cleansing ritual, immersing myself in a water shower. Once my ablutions have been meticulously performed, a sense of tranquillity and contentment shall envelop my being, rendering the world around me harmonious and pleasing.

And so it was that I uncorked the initial vessel. It proved to be an irresistible assemblage of elements. This veritable concatenation captivated my senses. The ancient spectre, concealed within the depths of my consciousness, stirred from its slumber, alluringly beckoning, beseeching for an augmented offering. I ventured to uncork a second vessel, desiring to ascertain whether the libation I had recently imbibed possessed the requisite potency of spirits. My conviction in its alcoholic nature had not yet been firmly established. At that moment, a sudden revelation seized hold of my consciousness: what if I were to partake in a small sip from each of these bottles? I shall deftly substitute the cork, rendering it imperceptible to all observers. It bore the semblance of an act akin to obliterating a dam, all in the pursuit of quenching the thirst of a meagre arid terrain! The torrent surged forth, an unstoppable force of nature, defying all attempts to quell its relentless power. In the realm of recollections, my dear mother - may the benevolence of Allah forever grace her soul - would often impart her wisdom with a touch of whimsy. She would utter, "Behold, the tail of the canine, subjected to the relentless passage of four decades, was shaped into a slender reed; yet, upon its liberation, it remained forever askew!" What an extraordinary display of sagacity! Having emerged from the humble hamlet of 'Ouja, a place renowned for its acerbic disposition, it is inconceivable for me to aspire to a state of unwavering rectitude akin to that of a slender reed, is it not? To partake in such an act would be a grievous betrayal of my ancestral hamlet, whose mere appellation subtly hints at the profound depths of our collective, yet lamentable, fate.

Indeed, I find myself in a state of certainty... The dog's tail, alas, shall forever remain curved despite the passage of four millennia, a testament to the unyielding nature of its form.

Thus, I embarked upon an unrestrained frenzy, ceaselessly traversing the realms of excess until my very pores exuded the essence of spirits, replacing the perspiration of toil. I staggered with a tantalising exhilaration, revelling in the merciless plundering of my surroundings. I meandered and stumbled amidst the cluttered bottles, my balance precarious, surrendering myself unabashedly to debauchery's capricious and domineering spirit. The duration of my undignified indulgence eludes me. Yet, I remain a witness to my disgraceful meandering and faltering, my feeble attempts to navigate the staircase, and my feeble attempts to traverse the kitchen floor, clutching tightly to a bottle. I then proceeded to stumble along the corridor, much to the dismay of the maid, who, though more frightened than astonished by my presence, endeavoured to assist me in regaining my composure.

It was not a sight that would have been deemed particularly pleasant to behold, I must confess. Burdened by the weight of her frail shoulders, the maid deemed it her solemn obligation to escort me to my quarters. My corporeal presence proved too ponderous for her delicate frame to bear. In that instant, we found ourselves entangled, my hand clumsily seeking refuge around her slender waist, daring to venture further until it seemed, for a brief moment, that I was indulging in the intimate caress of her bosom. She, in turn, responded with a cacophony of incomprehensible exclamations, yet, if memory serves me right, she displayed no concern for the audacious and lascivious advances my surrogate hand was making. Yet, I found myself unable to proceed any further, not due to any resistance from the maid against my desires - in fact, I believe she even encouraged them - but rather due to my pitiful incapacity to reach the culmination.

Now, the bitter taste of regret consumes me. To conduct oneself in such a manner, a mere two strides removed from one's spouse, was inconsequential and verging on the criminal. Even the lowly maid harbours resentment towards me, as evidenced by her actions yesterday. This morning, she callously allowed me to endure the incessant barking of my pleas before deigning to respond. In that moment of our encounter, her gaze, once entwined with mine, swiftly averted as if veiled by a pretence of bashfulness. Her behaviour is quite peculiar indeed. In apparent guise, she laments my presence, for I abruptly halted at the precise juncture when she yearned for further engagement!

Such a spectacle of madness! In this modern epoch,

individuals are increasingly succumbing to the perils of self-oblivion. They have lost sight of their rightful positions within the intricate web of social stratification, oblivious to the barriers that confine us all and the imperative to pay deference to those of higher standing. Verily, they are subjected to the incessant clamour of radio and television transmissions, wherein speeches extolling the virtues of justice and equality resound ceaselessly. Alas, they remain utterly bereft of any inclination to question the veracity of such proclamations, a sentiment I, on the other hand, ardently embrace. In our land, the conduct of our politicians is marked by a certain skittishness. This trepidation stems from the precarious nature of our circumstances. For, you see, in countries such as ours, where the weight of illiteracy bears down upon the masses with an oppressive force, delivering speeches becomes a perilous endeavour.

Should democratic elections ever be orchestrated, the sheer magnitude of the ignorant would undoubtedly inundate the hallowed halls of Parliament, threatening to engulf the very essence of our governance. These incendiary catchphrases propagate the cultivation of inconsequential aspirations, which could prove deleterious to their well-being if one were to succumb to their integrity. Consider, if you will, the lowly maid who casts upon her employer a gaze laden with base desire, yearning to partake in the intimate sanctuary of his bed. Should her audacity not falter, she may even dare to exploit his inebriation, seizing the opportunity to engage in a most unwelcome act of sexual harassment. In this perplexing realm of existence, I am compelled to inquire: to what destination are we traversing? Where, pray tell, does one find the elusive essence of respect? Where, pray tell, does one find the elusive nature of dignity?

Where, pray tell, does conscience reside? The elusive sense of religion, where does it live? Thankfully, the elusive concept of democracy shall forever remain an unattainable mirage within the confines of our beloved nation. In the face of this contemporary affliction that plagues the Western world, we have discovered an alluring remedy that cannot be resisted. Clean, fast, and efficient it is. In the realm of political tumult, a tempestuous military coup and the emergence of an enlightened despot are the requisite forces to quell and dismantle the treacherous aspirations of the unlettered masses. Thus, a Coup, regardless of its genesis, essence, and objectives, invariably proves to be beneficial for our collective well-being. President Abdelghani Abdelghaffar, with his dangerous squint, is the saviour we embrace.

***

Several months later

In a most fortunate turn of events, I find myself bestowed with the esteemed position of president within the ranks of the 'Ouja Islamic party's cell. This great honour was graciously granted to me by the illustrious General Abdelghani Abdelghaffar himself. I am compelled to assume the position once occupied by Hamda La'war. This situation represents the significant stature I have attained in the discerning gaze of our esteemed President. It is worth noting that upon learning of the successful quelling of the riots, courtesy of MY helicopters, the President promptly summoned me to his opulent palace.

When the telephone rang, its shrill cry pierced the air, interrupting the stillness of my solitude. I hesitated, my fingers trembling as they reached for the receiver, unsure of what awaited me on the other end of the line. It was Hassan, his voice dripping with a peculiar blend of mirth and mischief, as he regaled me with tidings that seemed too unbelievable to be true. Doubt crept into the recesses of my mind, whispering its scepticism, for I could not fathom that such joyous news could befall. In truth, I had not anticipated the bestowal of such a distinguished position within the confines of my ancestral hamlet. I conveyed my sentiments to him with conviction, leaving no room for doubt. A faint chuckle escaped his lips as he uttered, "You, my dear, deserve a more fitting recompense. Alas, such is the decree of our esteemed President."

The desire, nay, the earnest longing of the esteemed Mr. President! Why didn't he feel passionate about my getting a ministerial appointment? I wondered. With her persuasive charm, Sophia has concluded that I possess the qualities necessary to ascend to the lofty heights of statesmanship. She ceaselessly implores me to cease my nocturnal encounters with the bottles to awaken with a mind unburdened and brimming with brilliance. Ever since I chanced upon the mystical cavern akin to Ali Baba's treasure trove, I have succumbed to the peculiar habit of surrendering to the allure of Bacchus, spending countless hours in the dead of night, enraptured amidst towering heaps of bottles. In anticipation of the impending dawn, I would engage in the cleansing ritual, immersing myself in a bath, performing my ablutions meticulously, and embarking on a spiritual prayer journey. I persisted in my devotions, whether in the mosque's public embrace or my home's intimate confines. Yet, with her perplexed countenance, Sophia could not fathom the depths of my piety. Now, she has grown accustomed to it. However, we occasionally dispute, as she perceives my behaviour as paradoxical, inconsistent, and perhaps hypocritical.

Recently, she confided in me, saying: "Consult a psychiatrist for advice regarding your health concerns."

"For what purpose? I am not afflicted by madness."

"You aren't mad yet... But the time isn't right. Continued nightly partying with your extravagant religious rituals during the daytime could lead you to a mental institution."

"I cause no harm," I retorted. "Our business is thriving, and you should take comfort in the wealth we're accumulating. Our construction project is progressing well, with numerous other initiatives keeping us busy. The nationwide construction boom continues as we tackle challenges in every afflicted area. This ongoing celestial conflict is a blessing bestowed upon us. I cannot help but wish for it to last eternally. How fortunate we are with our abundant resources; what more could your heart desire? Besides, I have always fulfilled my duties as your spouse. What compels you to beseech my descent into madness? Don't I show you enough affection, my love, and am I not excessively devoted to you?"

Her laughter echoed through the room, a delicate symphony of joy that danced upon the air.

"Dear husband, please don't let infatuation with anyone other than me consume you. But your actions suggest a contradiction."

"Sophia, Sophia, haven't we covered this topic before? I've shared that this issue holds no anti-Islamic intent or contradiction. I find myself adopting the manners of historic caliphs. I've expressed my view that as we revive the magnificent Islamic era, it's natural and sensible to follow the practices of our venerated forebears. They often enjoyed beverages at night, then abstained once the Muezzin called, inviting the faithful to their religious duties. My dear, this is a tradition deeply rooted in my heart. You're familiar with my strong emotional bond to our ancestral customs. In what other way can I behave to show steadfast loyalty to that bygone era, which our wise Islamic leadership eagerly embraces?"

She stated that Hassan doesn't drink alcohol.

"I'm aware. In human perception, his statements have strayed from the truth. He finds it difficult to understand the deep meaning he aims to convey. The man, once a passionate preacher, has given up his pulpit. What is the gentleman doing at this moment? It's hard to say. Maybe, like me, he finds comfort in saving money to protect himself against the darkness that lies ahead. But the man, in his current state, seems to be doing well... Who knows, really?"

She wasn't surprised when I told her I'd been made president of the Ouja cell. She chuckled and said, "I see. That will help you rise from the underground, my dear. Politics can be complicated, but you'll become a governor eventually. Once you've taken on the role of Security Director, you'll be well on your way to becoming a Minister, that's for sure."

Despite learning about my demotion and transfer to Ouja in advance, I felt suspicious about her role in the decision despite being the one most affected. Given the president's ultimate authority in presidential aspirations, I couldn't refuse or challenge the appointment. It's essential to recognise that the president's wishes hold significant power.

In the opulent abode of Abdelghani Abdelghaffar, he graciously welcomed my presence. The duration of the interview was but a fleeting moment, a mere two or three minutes that passed with an ephemeral swiftness. Our exchange of words was but a quick and tenuous affair. Mamduh and Hassan found themselves amid a grand ceremony of decoration. With his peculiar manner of speech, the Minister half-swallowed his words and addressed the President thus: "Mis. President, there exists a certain businessman whose helicopters have played a significant role in quelling the riots."

Abdelghani emitted a low, guttural sound, manifesting his inner torment. The ocular orbs, concealed beneath the ebony frames, eluded my gaze.

"Welcome," he uttered, his voice a mere whisper in the vast expanse of the room.

He bore a striking resemblance to his posters, if not slightly diminished in authenticity, akin to a mere facsimile of his being.

Our hands met, a brief and perfunctory gesture of acknowledgement. The tumultuous surge of the historic moment engulfed me, rendering me breathless with its intoxicating allure. I found myself uttering in a halting manner, akin to the stammering of an uncertain soul: "Mr. President, your kind act is greatly appreciated." It is with great honour that I find myself in this particular circumstance, where I am compelled to express my sentiments... and so forth. Yet, I was unable to persist. The director of protocol delivered a small medallion carefully positioned upon a bed of lustrous fabric. Abdelghani placed the medal on my chest with a calm and skilled touch. His hands didn't tremble as he held it in position. He targeted my chest accurately, maintaining focus. With a graceful movement, he pinned the medal to my clothing, leaving me dressed in honour while the official who had given it remained nearby, ready to intervene if needed. Yet, the ceremony proved triumphant, and to this day, it remains an enigma to my perplexed mind. I still ponder the enigmatic manner in which he accomplished such a feat. In all honesty, I must confess my ignorance. The enchantment of authority, perchance, lies herein unless he had diligently honed his skills since the lamentable evasion of the Scoundrel!

Once more, our hands met in a firm clasp. He uttered these words with a solemnity that bespoke a deep-rooted admiration: "Today, Ouja takes pride in your achievements. You embody the qualities suitable for the presidency of its respected community."

His generosity was evident in how he chose to bestow upon me his flattering words. His remarks, like a delicate brushstroke upon the canvas of my soul, stirred within me a profound and ineffable sentiment. I was utterly moved, as if caught in the embrace of a gentle breeze, whispering secrets only the heart can comprehend. I stammered bashfully, offering my gratitude before departing. Soon after, Hassan trailed behind me, extending his congratulations and uttering: "Esteemed brother-in-law, this momentous occasion calls for celebration. Finally, you have ascended to the honourable status of a national hero."

"I must confess," I responded, "that it had forever been my heart's cherished desire."

After a few days had passed, I asked the young employee who had recently been appointed to take my place at the 'Ouja bank to come to my office, which was located in the secret heart of our party's cell. I didn't waste any time getting to the point and told him that his services were crucial to our cause. My words hung heavily in the air as I spoke.

To my astonishment, the youthful gentleman, whose demeanour exuded naivety and timidity, retorted with unexpected candour: "I am grateful for your offer, Mr. Bassam, but regretfully, I must decline as I am already employed at the bank."

In my contemplation, familiar laughter reached my ears, and a peculiar notion seized my mind. It dawned upon me that Hamda La'war, in his eternal resting place, was convulsing uncontrollably with mirth, his spirit consumed by a jealous derision directed towards none other than myself...

The end.

The first draft was finished in Tunis in December 1996 and 1997.

The last hand will be between London and Quillan (South France). April 2024.